Praise for

A LITTLE GENTLE SLEUTHING

'A first novel by a clearly gifted and knowledgeable writer, never less than engaging and readable'
Financial Times

FINISHING TOUCH

'Gently old-fashioned whodunit, riddled with lurking anguish'
The Times

OVER THE EDGE

'She has the rare skill that grabs the reader's complete attention at page one and holds it to the end'
Wilts and Gloucestershire Standard

EXHAUSTIVE ENQUIRIES

'The gently old-fashioned style of unravelling the mystery is as riveting as any violent fast-paced novel or film'
Cotswolds Life

MALICE POETIC

'Full of sharp insights with an unexpected twist in the tail. A satisfying read'
Val McDermid, *Manchester Evening News*

DEADLY LEGACY

'As absorbing as ever . . . another intriguing and dangerous case'
Gloucestershire Echo

Also by Betty Rowlands
and available from Hodder & Stoughton paperbacks

A Little Gentle Sleuthing
Finishing Touch
Over the Edge
Exhaustive Enquiries
Malice Poetic

About the author

In 1988 Betty Rowlands won the Sunday Express/ Veuve Clicquot Crime Short Story of the Year Competition. Her success continued with the publication of seven Melissa Craig Mysteries the most recent of which, *Smiling at Death*, is available from Hodder & Stoughton in hardcover. She is an active member of the Crime Writers' Association and regularly gives talks and readings, runs workshops and serves on panels at Crime Writing Conventions.

She lives in the heart of the Cotswolds where her Melissa Craig Mysteries are set and has three grown-up children and four grandchildren.

Deadly Legacy

Betty Rowlands

NEW ENGLISH LIBRARY
Hodder and Stoughton

Copyright © 1995 by Betty Rowlands

First published in Great Britain in 1995
by Hodder & Stoughton

First published in paperback in 1996
by Hodder & Stoughton
A division of Hodder Headline PLC

A New English Library paperback

The right of Betty Rowlands to be identified as the Author of
the Work has been asserted by her in accordance with the
Copyright, Designs and Patents Act 1988.

10 9 8 7 6 5 4 3 2

ISBN 0 340 64730 2

Printed and bound in Great Britain by
Cox & Wyman Ltd, Reading, Berkshire

Hodder and Stoughton
A division of Hodder Headline PLC
338 Euston Road
London NW1 3BH

To Jacintha Alexander
who pointed me in the right direction

Chapter One

Shortly before dawn, a light shower of snow fell on the Cotswold Hills. It formed an icy coating on leafless branches and the tops of dry-stone walls, and lay on ploughed fields like a scattering of sugar on chocolate cake. The day advanced, but still the snow remained, sparkling defiance at the late November sun.

On the roof of a pair of stone cottages snuggling against a bank on the outskirts of the village of Upper Benbury, circles bare of snow at the base of each chimney proclaimed that log fires within had succeeded where the sun had failed. Twin plumes of smoke rose into the frosty air, blue on blue against the winter sky.

Two women, returning with reddened cheeks and nipped toes and fingers from their walk along the valley footpath, scrambled over the wooden stile that bridged a gap in a hawthorn hedge and paused for a few moments to admire their homes: Hawthorn Cottage and Elder Cottage, owned respectively by Melissa Craig, successful crime writer, and Iris Ash, internationally acclaimed water-colourist and fabric designer.

A blackbird, foraging among a pile of dead leaves in Melissa's garden, appeared undisturbed by their arrival, but a flock of chaffinches burst in a whirring mass from an apple tree and went dipping and darting up the bank ahead of them. The birds' departure was watched with close attention by a half-Persian cat crouching under the hedge, ears cocked, fluffy tail twitching.

'Binkie-boy, come to Muvver!' called Iris and the cat yawned, rose, stretched and condescended to approach. 'Wozzee a cold boy in the snow, then?'

'The cottages look so pretty in this light, don't they? You ought to paint them,' said Melissa, doing her best not to show her irritation. Fond as she was of Iris, this habit of baby-talking to the cat set her teeth on edge.

Iris sniffed, partly in disdain, partly because the cold made her nose run. She took out a handkerchief and plied it vigorously before replying dismissively, 'Been done to death. Christmas card designs not my scene.'

'It'd be nice to keep as a reminder. You don't often see the place at this time of year.'

Iris shivered. 'Thank goodness. Not that it's been that mild in the Midi the past couple of years. Think I'll winter in the Algarve if it goes on.'

'Well, I'm really glad you're going to be at home this Christmas. My in-laws are going to a hotel for a change and they invited me to join them, but I wasn't keen. As you're not going to France, it gave me a good excuse to say "No".'

Iris's expression softened and she gave Melissa an affectionate pat on the shoulder before scooping Binkie into her arms and heading for her own front door. 'I'm going in. Getting cold, standing here gawping.'

'Me too, and I'm ready for some lunch. Come and have a bowl of soup with me?'

'What sort?' Iris, a passionate vegetarian, looked dubious.

'Carrot, lentil and tomato. No meat stock in it, I promise you.'

'Okay, thanks.'

In the porch of Hawthorn Cottage the two discarded their boots, scarves, gloves and anoraks before heading for the warm kitchen. Binkie made a beeline for his favourite spot beside the Aga; Iris perched on a stool and scanned the previous day's edition of the local paper while Melissa put a pan of soup to warm through and set bread, cheese and pickles on the table.

'Nasty business, this,' commented Iris, holding up the *Gazette* and pointing to the front page, which bore the headline *'STOWBRIDGE SEX STRANGLER'S LATEST VICTIM'*.

'Very nasty,' Melissa agreed with a shudder. 'One always thinks of Stowbridge as a quiet, sleepy little place.' She sighed. 'Nowhere's quiet and sleepy these days.'

'Not even Upper Benbury,' Iris agreed. She scanned the report, which ran to several columns. 'Three victims to date, all with the same story – a masked man grabs them by the throat and they pass out. Next thing they know, they're being indecently assaulted.' She pulled a face. 'Filthy pervert. Has your PC Plod got any leads?'

'If you mean DCI Harris . . .' Melissa began in mild exasperation, then caught the provocative gleam in her friend's eye and bit back an indignant retort. 'Not so far as I know. The attacker is always dressed entirely in black, wears a balaclava and never speaks, so there isn't even a voice description. They think it must be someone with medical knowledge because he knows where to apply pressure to make the victims lose consciousness almost immediately – but so does almost anyone who's done a first aid course. So far he hasn't seriously injured any of them, but it must be a ghastly experience to wake up and find yourself bound and gagged and . . .' Melissa shuddered at the picture she had conjured up.

'Quite ghastly,' Iris agreed.

'What worries the police most of all is that one day this creature will get it wrong and kill someone. They're desperate to catch him.'

'Hope they do.' Iris turned to the inside pages of the paper. 'I see Bruce Ingram is back with the *Gazette*,' she remarked.

'Really?' Melissa glanced up from the loaf she was slicing. 'Last I heard of him, he was in the police force.'

'Must have quit. Still waging war on corruption, though. Seen this piece about dodgy planning decisions?'

'As a matter of fact, I haven't opened a newspaper for the past three days. I've been working flat out on my new novel.'

'How's it going?'

'Finished, except for the final read-through. The soup's nearly ready – anything else of interest before we eat?'

'Not much – charity fun-runs and pub brawls.' Iris turned another page, ran her eyes over the headlines and exclaimed, 'Oh, no!'

'Now what?'

'You met Leonora Jewell, didn't you?'

'Yes, at a book signing a few months ago. What about her?'

'Been found dead. Here.' Iris held out the paper and pointed. Mechanically continuing to stir her soup, Melissa read aloud the brief report, which was headed:

WRITER'S BODY FOUND IN ISOLATED COTTAGE.

The body of Miss Leonora Jewell, the best-selling novelist, was found yesterday morning in the living room of her cottage on the outskirts of Lower Southcote. Detective Inspector Holloway of Stowbridge CID stated that there were signs of forced entry and it is thought Miss Jewell may have disturbed an intruder. 'The cause of death is not yet known,' said DI Holloway. 'Our enquiries are continuing.'

'Poor old Leonora,' said Melissa with a frown and a sympathetic shake of the head.

4

'Was she old?'

'She must have been pushing eighty, but you'd never have thought it. She was only a little thing, but she had a very authoritative manner and a voice like a games mistress. She was the sort to go for a burglar with a poker if she caught one in her house.'

'Maybe she did, and he had a go back.'

'Maybe. It's the sort of thing Ken Harris is forever warning me against.'

'Don't take much notice, do you?' said Iris with a wry grin. Melissa grinned back at the oblique reference to the narrow squeaks she had experienced when dabbling in amateur sleuthing, despite the efforts of Detective Chief Inspector Harris to discourage such adventures.

'I've never attacked anyone,' she protested. 'And I don't *mean* to get into dodgy situations, it just happens. It sure does help with plots, though,' she added as she ladled the thick, spicy broth into bowls. 'Help yourself to bread.'

For a few minutes they ate in silence. Then Melissa said, 'I wonder if Joe Martin's heard about Leonora.'

'Your agent? Does he know her?'

'She's one of his authors. He'll miss her like hell . . . her books make mega-bucks for him.'

'Make even more now,' Iris remarked, reaching for another piece of bread. 'Nothing like violent death for boosting sales.'

'You old cynic!'

'Realist,' Iris corrected. 'What sort of books did she write?'

'Family sagas, I believe. I've never read any of them, but quite a few have been filmed. Her fans will be shocked to hear about her death.'

The tragedy, coupled with the series of unpleasant sex attacks on young women, had a sobering effect on the two friends. For a while their conversation centred on the risks involved in choosing to live in isolated dwellings and the precautions they had both taken to make their own homes secure. They then turned to other, more congenial topics.

It did not occur to either of them that this was no ordinary burglary.

Chapter Two

A couple of days later, Melissa was strolling along the Promenade in Cheltenham, gazing into shop-windows dressed for the festive season and telling herself that it was time she gave some serious thought to Christmas shopping. She was in a buoyant mood, having just despatched her completed manuscript to Joe Martin, and was for the first time in a month under no pressure to go home and settle down to work. So she dawdled among the hurrying crowds, enjoying the winter sunshine, pausing for a few minutes to listen to a young violinist who had set up a music stand beside the main entrance to the town's largest store and was giving a creditable rendering of Bach's 'Air on the G String'. When the piece was finished, Melissa dropped a coin in the open violin case lying on the ground; the girl smiled and thanked her as she re-tuned her instrument and flipped over the pages of her score.

Melissa sauntered on. She bought freshly-roasted coffee beans in a shop on the corner opposite the Town Hall, crossed the road and came to the Imperial Gardens, neat and tidy as always, although the summer displays of flowers had long since been cleared away and replaced by wallflowers and polyanthus not yet in bloom. The café was closed, its tables and chairs stored away for the winter, but one or two shoppers, thankful no doubt for the opportunity to set down their burdens, sat on wooden benches and basked in the unseasonal warmth. It was hard to believe that, only a day or two previously, the trees and lawns had been encrusted with frost.

Melissa had parked her car on the far side of the square. She had just reached it and was unlocking the driver's door when she became aware of another car pulling up a short distance behind her. Someone waiting for her to drive off so that he or she could take the vacated space, no doubt. She put her bag on the back seat and was about to get in when someone grabbed her elbow. She let out a gasp of alarm.

'You're nicked!' said a familiar voice. 'Better come quietly.'

'Ken! You scared the life out of me!' she scolded, trying to sound annoyed, but unable to hide her pleasure at seeing him.

'Sorry.' The lumpy features of Detective Chief Inspector Kenneth Harris of Gloucestershire CID crumpled like a relief map of the Cotswolds as he grinned down at her. 'Consider it a punishment for the anxiety you've been causing me for the past few days. What have you been doing, Mel? I've been worried about you.'

'Working. I told you, I was finishing a book.'

'You could have answered the phone. I've been calling and calling . . .'

'I unplugged it. Every time it rings, it upsets my train of thought.'

'That's not fair. You might at least have left the answering machine switched on.'

'It still disturbs me. It was only for a few days, while I did my final revision.'

'Well, at least I've found you again. Have you had lunch?'

'Not yet. I was just on my way home.'

'Then let's go and grab a bite. Wait here – I'll tell Waters to pick me up in an hour.' The big detective strode off to speak to his sergeant, who was still waiting with his engine running. Returning in a couple of minutes, he took Melissa firmly by the arm as if afraid she would make a break for it.

'I feel as if I'm being arrested,' she protested, trying not to reveal how much she was enjoying the sensation.

'You are,' he assured her. 'You're going down for a stiff sentence.' She stopped in her tracks and hooted with mirth at the unintended *double entendre*. 'Woman, you have a disgusting mind,' he said. 'I've a good mind to take you home and bed you without any lunch.'

Melissa feigned dismay. 'No, please, I'm starving,' she pleaded.

'All right. A stay of execution is granted. How about a pizza?'

'Great.'

It was early and the pizzeria was almost empty. They found a corner table and Harris gave their order. While they were waiting, he leaned forward and laid a large, reddish hand over one of Melissa's. 'You know, Mel, I was concerned about you,' he said earnestly. 'In fact, I rang Iris to check you were okay.'

'Really? She never said.'

'I asked her not to. I knew you'd get tetchy.'

'I don't get tetchy,' she said indignantly, then giggled as she caught his eye. 'All right, now and again, but only when I'm under pressure.'

'It's because of what happened to Leonora Jewell that I got anxious,' he explained. 'She lived in the same sort of out-of-the-way place as you and Iris.'

'Yes, I know.' The thought sobered them both. 'Have you got anyone for that?'

He pursed his lips and shook his head. 'It's not going to be easy. The old lady was a very private person . . . lived alone, rarely had visitors, no close relatives or friends except her godson, who lives in Cardiff and only visited occasionally. We don't even know for certain what's been stolen, apart from a carriage clock, a portable radio and whatever cash was in her handbag. There's a help who's been coming in a couple of days a week – she's the one who found the body – but she's not been able to tell us much.'

'Was there a struggle?'

'We think there may have been. She died of a fractured skull, probably sustained when she fell and hit her head on the stone hearth, but we aren't sure exactly what happened or what caused the fall. She might have had a heart attack – the pathologist is carrying out further tests.'

'And, presumably, there were no witnesses?'

'We haven't found any so far. The cottage is tucked away, out of sight from the road. We've appealed for anyone who was in the area at the time to come forward, but there's been no useful response to date.'

'Anything new on the "Sex Strangler"?'

'We're piecing something together, but clues are thin on the ground there as well. We picked up a suspect who answered the description – such as it is, he doesn't give much away – but we had to let him go for lack of evidence. We'll get him in the end, but it could take time and meanwhile the women in Stowbridge are terrified to go out alone at night.'

He broke off as a young waiter approached with their food. For a few minutes they ate without speaking. Then Harris said in a lower tone than before, 'There's something about Leonora Jewell's death that's bugging me.'

'What?'

He chewed thoughtfully on a forkful of pizza before replying, 'On the face of it, it's just another break-in, probably by some unemployed kids. We get similar cases every week; they target an area, do several houses in quick succession and then move on. I think that's what seems odd about this one; there haven't been any other incidents reported in Lower Southcote for several months, and nothing since. Why pick on her? Although she must have made a fortune from her books, she lived very simply, and so far as we've been able to make out, the cottage contained very little of value to a petty thief. No TV, no video or CD player – that's what those characters are mainly after.'

'But it is isolated, and presumably easy to break into?'

'Yes, but others in the village are equally vulnerable and offer much richer pickings. A lot of the people are out all day and security's low – there's not even a Neighbourhood Watch there.'

They finished their meal. Harris checked the time.

'Sorry, I have to go now. Duty calls and all that.' He paid the bill and they walked back to where Melissa had left her car. He took her key, unlocked the door and held it open. 'This evening?' he said, his eyes locked onto hers.

'Come for supper – about seven?'

'Fine.'

'I was going to call you,' she said, as if by way of an apology.

'Okay, you're forgiven.'

His expression told her that he very much wanted to kiss her, but she knew he would not. Not now, not here, not in public. In his way, he too was a private person. And there was the whole evening to look forward to.

Chapter Three

The following morning, Melissa had a call from Joe Martin.

'Thanks for the script,' he said. 'I'm looking forward to reading it.'

'I'm glad it arrived safely – I'm so thankful to be shot of it. I'm not going to write another line for the rest of this year.'

'Er . . . that's something I want to talk to you about.'

'Joe, I have a feeling you're going to spring something unwelcome on me.'

'It's nothing too onerous . . . I mean, it shouldn't take long,' he said hurriedly. 'It's just . . . well, there's this editor making urgently persuasive noises and if I could just come up with what she wants . . . quickly . . .'

'Do stop waffling and get to the point,' said Melissa impatiently. 'But before you do,' she added, 'I'd like to make it clear that I'm doing no signings this side of the holiday, nor am I judging Christmas story competitions for the kiddie-winkies.'

'It's nothing like that.'

'Then what?'

'It's about Leonora Jewell.' There was a short silence; she sensed that he was searching for the right approach. Or was he doing it to arouse her curiosity? She waited.

'You know she was murdered by an intruder?' he said at last.

'Who said it was murder?'

'Unlawfully killed, then – what's the difference?'

'About twenty years, I think. And there's been no inquest yet, so . . .'

'Let's not bother with technicalities. The point is, she's shuffled off this mortal coil leaving an unfinished script and a deadline only a couple of months away.'

'Do I understand you're trying to get me to ghost a Leonora Jewell saga?' Melissa exclaimed. Really, she thought, the cheek of the man!

'It's a departure from her usual style . . . more of a mystery novel really . . . nearer your kind of thing . . . and I believe it's only missing the last three chapters. I've got her plot outline . . . it wouldn't take long . . . not to a professional like you.' His voice became progressively more oleaginous.

'Spare me the flannel. You said you *believe* it's only missing the last three chapters. Is that what she told you?'

'We spoke on the phone a few days before she was mur . . . before she died. She was confident she'd have the thing finished in good time.'

'Well, I don't know. I'm not too keen on the idea. I really was looking forward to a rest.'

'*Please*.' Now he was trying cajolery. 'We're promised quite a hefty share in the advance and a percentage of the royalties.'

'You mean you've already been discussing the details? You might have consulted me first.'

'I was approached by Leonora's publisher. It's her hundredth book and they've been planning a big launch, with national media coverage and all that. They'll lose heavily if the script isn't ready on time.'

'And you agreed, just like that?'

'I was pretty sure I could count on you.'

'I don't believe I'm hearing this. It didn't occur to you I might be planning to take off for the Caribbean tomorrow?'

'Good Lord, you're not, are you?' He sounded so alarmed

14

that Melissa almost laughed aloud. 'Don't let me down, Mel,' he pleaded. 'There's big money in it . . . Leonora's sales are astronomical . . . they'll shoot up more than ever now, of course . . .'

'And you don't want to lose out on your commission.' Joe's preoccupation with the bottom line was a regular target for Melissa's sarcasm. 'Okay, I'll think about it.'

'Good girl. I've arranged a meeting tomorrow with Leonora's executor, who's her godson, by the way. I've already spoken to her solicitor, who sees no reason why he should object to our visiting the cottage and collecting the script . . .'

'Just a minute,' Melissa broke in. 'Did you say *our* visiting the cottage?'

'Well, I naturally thought you'd want to see where she worked . . . get the atmosphere and all that . . . and of course you'll have to check what research material you'll need and so on.'

The switch from conditional to simple future did not escape her. 'You take one hell of a lot for granted, Joe Martin.'

'But you'll do it?'

'I've told you, I'm not . . .'

'My appointment to meet the executor at the solicitor's office is at ten o'clock tomorrow morning. I'm sure I can change the time if it doesn't suit you, and meanwhile, I'll fax you the *Deadly Legacy* plot outline. The office is in Imperial Square, Cheltenham.'

Mechanically, Melissa jotted down the address. She could not help being intrigued by the assignment, but irritation at the arbitrary way she had virtually been committed without prior consultation made her decide to keep Joe dangling a little longer.

'All right,' she said at length, '*If* I decide to take it on, I'll meet you there. But I'm *not promising*,' she added, and put down the telephone before he could argue further.

Mr Semple, senior partner in the old established firm of Rathbone and Semple, Solicitors, was a little below average height, slim and wiry-looking, clean shaven with thinning iron-grey hair. His demeanour as he welcomed Melissa and Joe to the mahogany-and-dark-leather gloom of his office, with its high ceilings, narrow windows and walls lined with legal tomes, was courteous but brisk. Melissa had the impression that here was a man who knew his job and did not suffer fools gladly.

Joe Martin was already there when she arrived, together with a tall, spare individual with bloodless features and hollow cheeks who was introduced as Jonathan Round, godson and executor to the late Leonora Jewell. He extended a bony hand with an expression of studied solemnity which aroused in Melissa – still a shade resentful at being manoeuvred into this situation – a perverse desire to shock him. Observing his lean frame, she was almost tempted into making a wisecrack about the inappropriateness of his name, but refrained out of consideration for Joe, who was shooting nervous glances in her direction like a parent fearing his offspring was about to say or do something outrageous.

'Mr Semple is going to accompany us to Miss Jewell's cottage,' announced Mr Round, without noticeable enthusiasm. 'I've travelled from Cardiff by train, so he has offered his services as chauffeur.'

'It seems we're putting you to a great deal of trouble, Mr Round,' said Joe, rather unctuously, Melissa thought.

'Not at all. As my godmother's executor I am, you will appreciate, responsible for the disposal of her property in accordance with her wishes, once probate of her will has been granted. Until then, I'm personally responsible for its safety,' he explained.

'You needn't worry, we're not planning to pinch the spoons,' said Melissa, before she could stop herself. 'Are we Joe?'

Joe winced, Mr Round looked pained and Mr Semple's mouth twitched at the corners. Melissa could not be sure, but she thought she detected a passing twinkle in his bright blue eyes. It was gone in a flash – he was, after all, receiving them in his professional capacity – but she sensed that, to a certain extent at any rate, he shared her feelings about his client.

'I'm not suggesting that you will do anything of the kind,' said Mr Round stiffly. 'I'm merely making my position clear. My godmother has bequeathed her manuscripts to the Faculty of English at the University of New England.'

'But until probate has been granted,' Mr Semple interposed, 'they will remain where she arranged for them to be kept before her death, namely in my firm's strongroom. Her instructions on this point are made clear in the will. I have the formalities in hand, of course, but it will be some weeks before they are complete.'

'I am sure you will do your best to expedite matters, Mr Semple,' said Mr Round.

'Naturally, Mr Round,' said Mr Semple.

That there was latent animosity between the two men was plain. Melissa decided to take the initiative before it broke the surface.

'Well, Mr Semple,' she said briskly. 'Are there any legal matters we have to discuss before we go to Miss Jewell's cottage? I take it Mr Martin has, er, declared our interest?'

'Oh yes, we discussed the publisher's proposal in some detail before you arrived and Mr Round is prepared to allow you reasonable access to Miss Jewell's, er, work in progress.' Semple's glance swivelled briefly towards Round, who gave a dignified nod. 'I must say,' he went on, 'as an admirer of your books, Mrs Craig, I can think of no one better fitted to undertake this sad task.'

'You've very kind, thank you,' said Melissa sincerely. 'I take it nothing has been removed from Miss Jewell's files?'

'Indeed, no. In fact, permission to enter the premises was granted by the police only two days ago . . .'

'I immediately authorised the cleaning woman to go in and tidy things up,' interrupted Mr Round, as if determined not to have his authority undermined. 'The police left the place in a terrible mess.'

'Shall we go, then?' said Melissa.

'By all means,' said Mr Semple. 'There's just one thing before we leave, Mrs Craig. Would you do one of my staff a favour?'

'Certainly.'

'She's an admirer of yours and she was most excited when she heard you were coming here. She has a number of your books – would you mind signing them for her?'

'It'd be a pleasure.'

'Thank you.' He pressed a button on his desk and when a woman's voice answered he said, 'Tell Carole she may come in now.'

A moment later there was a gentle knock on the door and a slight, fair-haired young woman with solemn eyes behind round spectacles came in with several well-thumbed paperbacks in her hands. She was flushed with embarrassment and her 'How do you do, Ms Craig?' as Mr Semple introduced her was a shy whisper. She watched with shining eyes as Melissa dedicated and signed each book.

'Thank you so much, it's really kind of you,' she said, and backed out of the office as if from the presence of royalty.

'You've really made her day,' said Mr Semple. 'She's seen every televised episode of your books as well.'

'She's probably got a crush on Gareth Huntingdon,' said Melissa with a chuckle. 'The actor who plays my detective, Nathan Latimer,' she explained, as he looked blank.

'Ah, yes, quite so. Well, let us be on our way.' He got to his feet, put on his hat and coat and led the way out of his office. 'I'll go and get my car.'

'Mine's parked just up the road. I'll follow you along,' said Melissa.

'Very well. I'll meet you gentlemen outside.' He disappeared along a passage, leaving the others to make their way to the front door.

Mr Round hung back to speak to the receptionist and Joe seized the opportunity to hiss in Melissa's ear, 'Stop giving him aggro or he might change his mind about letting you work on Leonora's script.'

'Aggro?' Melissa assumed an innocent expression. 'All I did was make a harmless jest . . .'

'Can't you see, the man has no sense of humour?'

'You're right. He's a pompous jackass.'

'Never mind that. He's got the power to deny us access to her papers if he's so minded.'

'And that would lose us lots of lovely money, right?'

'It isn't just the money . . .'

'No?'

'It's a matter of not disappointing the fans . . .'

'Oh, of course.'

'Shh, here he comes. Please, Mel.'

At the sight of his anguished expression, she relented. 'All right, I promise I'll be good.'

Chapter Four

Quarry Cottage lay at the end of a narrow track that snaked downhill from the main road into Stowbridge, half a mile or so from the village of Lower Southcote. The road continued straight on for a short distance before doubling back on itself to hide below a steep bank, which prevented passers-by – even those on horseback – from catching a glimpse of the small stone dwelling in the valley. The village was scarcely more than a hamlet, perched on a hilltop like something out of a child's picture-book, its tiny church one of the smallest in the county.

The cottage was shabby, almost decrepit in appearance, with paint peeling from the door and window frames, gaps in the fence and broken tiles on the roof. As she walked with the three men along a mossy path to the front door, Melissa reflected that very little of the substantial sums reputedly earned by Leonora Jewell's ninety-nine novels had been spent on the upkeep of her property. The garden, however, was in perfect order, having been planted and tended with knowledge and love. Evergreen shrubs made a foil for the soft pastels of wintersweet, jasmine and laurestinus; bright ruby, white and amethyst heathers lined the path on either side. There was a stone bird-bath on a pedestal in the middle of the front lawn and half a coconut swung from an apple tree, where two bluetits, greedily feasting, darted away at the visitors' approach.

'It's perfect – like something out of a gardening magazine,' Melissa exclaimed.

'A picture, isn't it?' agreed Mr Semple. 'Except for the heavy jobs like tree pruning, she did it all herself.'

The temperature indoors was lower than outside and the place smelt of disinfectant. It was, Melissa thought, almost like entering a mortuary; instinctively, she hung back to let the others go first as, with a brisk command of 'This way, please,' Mr Round led them along the narrow hallway, opened a door and ushered them into an oak-beamed, low-ceilinged room with windows at either end.

'Miss Jewell used this as a combined sitting-room and study,' he informed them. 'The working area is over there.' He waved a hand towards an alcove overlooking the rear garden, containing a plain wooden desk, some bookshelves and a battered metal filing cabinet. 'All her books and papers are exactly as she left them. Here's the key to the cabinet, where you'll find the script of her current novel.'

'I expect you'd like to spend a little time browsing, Melissa,' said Joe. 'Why don't we' – he glanced from one to the other of their companions – 'leave you in peace for a while? I noticed a pub in the village – we could have a drink and find out if they can do us some lunch later on.'

'Good idea,' said Mr Semple.

'You go by all means,' said Mr Round. 'I'll stay here in case Mrs Craig wishes to ask any questions.' Without waiting for confirmation, he sat down in an armchair and lit a cigarette.

Melissa glared at him. Out of the corner of her eye, she saw a look of apprehension on Joe's face, but ignored it. 'You're familiar with Miss Jewell's work, I take it, Mr Round?' she said icily.

'Not at all,' he replied. 'I seldom read novels.' He sounded

22

offended, as if he had been accused of studying pornography. 'I'm here in my capacity as her executor.'

'And I'm here in *my* capacity as a writer who has been invited to complete her unfinished novel,' Melissa informed him, 'and when I'm working I find it impossible to concentrate with anyone else in the room. If I'm going to take on this job, I must insist on being left alone for a while. You needn't worry, I'm not in the business of plagiarism.'

Mr Round appeared taken aback, Mr Semple was seized with a fit of coughing and Joe, looking more anguished by the second, said nervously, 'I assure you, Mr Round, I can vouch for Mrs Craig's utter integrity.'

'I don't need anyone to vouch for me, thank you very much,' Melissa said coolly. 'But if Mr Round insists on a character reference, he can contact Detective Chief Inspector Kenneth Harris of the county CID.' If she was blowing the whole thing, she didn't care. She didn't really want the job anyway.

Mr Round was looking increasingly uncomfortable and it dawned on her that he was much younger than she had at first thought. She had mentally put him down as approaching forty; now she realised that it was his air of solemn superiority that had misled her. It could have been a façade, to conceal a lack of experience, to maintain his self-esteem before a professional man many years his senior. In the face of her attack, he had lost much of his confidence and appeared chastened and ill at ease. She began to feel sorry for him.

He heaved his lanky frame out of the chair. 'I assure you, I had no intention . . . I didn't mean . . . I'm sorry if I seemed to imply . . .' he stammered. 'Of course, if you want us to leave, Mrs Craig . . .' His voice trailed away and he made a great show of looking for somewhere to deposit the ash from his cigarette, finally tapping it into his cupped hand.

Melissa rewarded his capitulation with a gracious smile. 'Why don't you leave the key, to save you the trouble of coming back to lock up?' she purred.

Meekly, he took a small leather case from his pocket and handed it over. Behind him, Melissa spotted Mr Semple smirking and Joe looking so aghast at what he doubtless saw as her effrontery that she had difficulty in keeping a straight face. The three men moved towards the door; she undertook to join them for lunch at the Ploughman's Arms and they departed, leaving her in temporary possession of the field.

She did not immediately settle down to work, but spent several minutes studying her surroundings. The interior of the cottage, although perfectly neat and tidy, gave no more indication of the owner's undoubted wealth than the exterior. The heavy velvet curtains were faded, the furniture comfortable but shabby. The focal point of the room was a Cotswold stone chimney-piece of the type found in hundreds of cottages in the area, often featuring – surrounded by horse-brasses and copper kettles, with gun-dogs dozing in front of log fires – in glossy magazines dedicated to country living. In this simple dwelling there were few ornaments – none of any apparent value – and no trace of an open fire; instead, a portable gas heater stood on the cold hearth, which was made of several stone slabs a good two inches thick. Melissa's stomach twitched uneasily at the sight of a stain on the edge of the carpet. Was that the spot where Leonora Jewell had crashed to the floor, shattering her skull? Had she foolishly grappled with the intruder, or suffered a heart-attack from shock at coming face to face with him? Was it possible the fall had been unconnected with the burglary and merely the result of a sudden loss of balance? And what exactly had the intruder been after? Judging from the state of her home, Leonora had accumulated very few material possessions. Melissa found herself echoing Ken Harris's question: Why had the thief picked on her?

She went into the passage and found the kitchen. The back door was locked, but she quickly identified the key, opened it and stepped outside. The small back garden, like the front, was a delight, with more winter-flowering shrubs and a holly tree sparkling with berries. It was easy to picture the elderly writer working away at her desk in the alcove, looking up from time to time to rest her eyes and enjoy her small, secluded paradise.

Melissa stepped back inside and relocked the door, noticing as she did so that one pane of glass had been recently replaced. The putty was still soft and the glazier's fingermarks had not been removed. So that was how the intruder had got in. The key had probably been in the lock at the time, easy to reach and turn.

Like the sitting-room, the kitchen held few luxuries, apart from a washing machine, a microwave oven and a small freezer – essential for anyone living in this isolated spot and liable to be cut off in bad weather for days on end. A single cupboard held basic groceries, a few items of crockery and a couple of saucepans; Leonora had spent little time on food preparation. Melissa took a peek into the freezer and saw a stack of ready-prepared meals. She had a momentary, but vivid, flash of insight into the dead woman's lifestyle, her waking hours divided between the desk where she wrote her best-selling sagas and the garden she had tended with so much care.

The time was slipping past. Melissa returned to the chilly sitting-room, found a box of matches and lit the gas fire. She unlocked the cabinet; in the top drawer were a number of suspension files, neatly labelled and evidently containing correspondence. In the second drawer she found two bulky pocket folders marked 'Deadly Legacy'. She took them to the desk, pushed aside the battered manual typewriter and settled down to read.

She had already studied the plot outline that Joe had faxed her. It was a Gothic mystery concerning a missing heiress, some old masters of dubious authenticity, a priceless stolen painting and a series of unexplained deaths, set in Victorian times – almost, she thought as she read on, a pastiche of a Wilkie Collins novel. She skimmed through the first two chapters, compared them with the outline and found they corresponded in all but a few unimportant details. Leonora Jewell had been a meticulous plotter. The style was colourful but straightforward and would, she decided, be fairly simple to imitate. She would have to do some background reading to get the period atmosphere right, but that presented no difficulty either, as the author had compiled a short bibliography and the books listed were on the shelf at her elbow. She calculated that the three unwritten chapters represented between fifteen and twenty thousand words. She would have her work cut out to finish the job within two months. Ken Harris would not be best pleased.

It was one o'clock and she was beginning to feel hungry. She relocked the filing cabinet and put the reference books and the folders containing the manuscript into a shopping bag she found in the kitchen. Then she turned off the gas fire and went out, locking the front door behind her.

Returning to her car, she noticed something she had not spotted on the way in: a low, circular stone structure covered by a heavy wooden lid, evidently an old well. There was nothing unusual about that; there were wells in the gardens of several cottages in Upper Benbury, most of them disused and capped with metal grilles for safety.

Melissa would never understand what prompted her, after stowing the bag behind the driver's seat, to go back, remove the ancient wooden lid and peer inside. This was a well that had presumably run dry, for it had been filled with rocks and rubble to within a couple of feet of ground level.

Lying on top of the stones was a short length of angle iron. Without thinking, she reached down and retrieved it. One end bore traces of a dried, brown substance to which clung a tuft of white hair.

Chapter Five

The lounge bar of the Ploughman's Arms was warm, crowded and buzzing with seasonal goodwill. As Melissa stood inside the swing door, her eyes seeking her three companions, her mind was still on her gruesome discovery. She had no doubt whatsoever that what she had held in her hand only a few minutes ago was the weapon that had killed Leonora Jewell.

Throughout the short drive from Quarry Cottage she had been trying to decide what to do. Her instinct was to find the nearest telephone and contact Ken Harris, to tell him she had stumbled upon proof – or at any rate, a strong indication – that his misgivings about the burglary were justified. Who would deliberately strike down a defenceless old woman for the sake of a few oddments of more interest to the organiser of a jumble sale than a professional thief?

She had a strong suspicion, however, that if she were to take the initiative and contact the police directly, the professional pride of certain individuals would be seriously ruffled. Perhaps the correct course would be to inform Leonora's solicitor and executor, both of whom were present, and let them handle it. Or was it her duty to do something herself? Common sense told her that this shouldn't be a problem, but somehow she wasn't thinking clearly. She was still undecided as she approached the corner table where the three men sat, chatting over drinks and sandwiches.

They stood up when they saw her. Joe took his coat from a fourth chair and held it while she sat down. 'How did it go?' he asked eagerly.

'Very interesting,' she said guardedly. She turned to Mr Round. 'The script was in two folders and I've brought them and some books away with me to work on at home. I hope you have no objection?'

She half expected him to demur, but he said quietly, 'No, of course not. I really have no idea how you writers work, but Mr Martin has been telling me how professional you are.'

'You mustn't take too much notice of Joe,' said Melissa facetiously, partly in an effort to hide her suppressed agitation.

Mr Semple cleared his throat and said, 'I suggest that for the sake of order we ask Mrs Craig to sign a receipt for the items she has removed from the cottage.'

'Would that be all right?' asked Mr Round.

'Of course, no problem,' she assured them. She had a shrewd idea of the thought that lay behind Mr Semple's slightly condescending smile. *'I'll teach that presumptuous puppy how things should be handled,'* it seemed to say.

Joe was still on his feet. 'What will you have?' he asked Melissa.

'I could murder a cup of coffee. I'm feeling a bit cold.' Despite the close atmosphere, she realised she was shivering.

'Didn't you light the gas fire?' asked Mr Round. 'I'm sorry, I should have done it for you . . .'

'It doesn't matter.' She wasn't ready yet to speak about her discovery or explain that, although Leonora's sitting-room had warmed up very quickly, she was unable to shake off the sensation of chill that had crept over her as she held the bloodstained weapon. She needed time to steady herself.

Mr Round's eagerness to be conciliatory was quite touching and she made an effort to respond to his change of attitude.

'Here are the keys – and I *did* remember to lock the front door,' she said, and he gave an embarrassed grin. She thought how much pleasanter he looked when he smiled.

Joe was still hovering at her elbow. 'What about something to eat?' he said.

'Oh, er, a sandwich will do.'

'Ham, cheese, egg . . . ?'

'Anything . . . whatever they have.' The prospect of food held no attraction at the moment. Joe gave her a searching look before going to the bar to give the order. *He knows I've got something on my mind*, she thought. *He's going to ask questions . . . I'd like to tell him first, without the others listening and staring . . .* In the hope of catching him on his own, she half rose to leave the table on the pretext of going to the toilet, but already he was swallowed up in the crowd round the bar. There would be no privacy there. So she sat and made small talk with the others until Joe returned with her coffee and sandwich. She drank half of the hot, stimulating drink, took a single bite from the sandwich and gagged on it.

'Something's upset you. What is it?' Joe demanded.

'I'm sorry, I can't eat a thing.' She pushed the plate away. The mental picture of Leonora Jewell lying fatally injured and bleeding on her own hearth, the victim of a vicious and cowardly attack, was too vivid; it had totally destroyed her appetite. The three men were looking at her with concern. 'I came across something that makes me believe Leonora's death wasn't accidental,' she said. She could hear the shakiness in her own voice.

In response to their shocked glances, she put down her cup and leaned forward over the table; the others did the same. In a low voice, making sure people at neighbouring tables could not overhear, she described her discovery.

'There's something odd about that break-in,' she finished.

'I'm not sure what it is, but . . . Leonora seemed such an unlikely target for a burglar.'

There was a brief silence. Mr Round looked perturbed, Joe merely intrigued. Mr Semple considered for several moments before saying gravely, 'I doubt if it was done by a professional. The intruder was more likely to have been a young opportunist who panicked and beat her up when she disturbed him.'

'She wasn't exactly beaten up, she suffered a single blow to the head,' Melissa pointed out. 'I've not heard yet . . .' She broke off, aware that she should not be revealing the extent of her knowledge of the case. What DCI Harris had told her was in confidence; it would do him no good if it became public knowledge that he indulged in indiscreet gossip. 'I mean, the police haven't released the result of the post-mortem, have they?' she said hastily.

Mr Round shook his head, frowning. 'I still can't agree that this indicates anything but a burglary that went horribly wrong,' he said emphatically.

'But nothing of value was taken,' she pointed out. 'In fact, there *was* nothing of value.'

'We can't be sure of that, can we?' Mr Semple pointed out. He glanced for confirmation at Mr Round, who merely shrugged and replied, 'I've no idea what she kept there. But – no, I suppose not.' Melissa's brain was beginning to buzz with questions she had no right to ask.

'We must leave everything in the hands of the police,' said the solicitor firmly. 'They must know of your discovery at once – it could be instrumental in tracking down this villain. May I assume you're happy to leave it to me, as Miss Jewell's legal adviser, to inform them?' His gaze swivelled briefly between Round and Melissa and they both nodded agreement. 'They will certainly wish to speak to you later, Mrs Craig, but I'll explain that you are too upset to talk about it just yet.'

Melissa gave him a grateful smile. 'That's very kind, thank you.' What he had said wasn't strictly true; she was feeling much steadier now that someone else had taken charge, and in any case she had on more than one occasion been interviewed while in a far greater state of shock. Still, there were times when it was nice to be treated in such a protective way. Joe Martin, please take note.

'I'll do it immediately from my cellphone.' Mr Semple took the instrument from his overcoat pocket and stood up. 'It's too noisy in here, and in any case we don't want the whole world to know. I'll make the call from my car.'

'You should try to eat something, Mrs Craig,' said Mr Round solicitously, as Mr Semple made his way across the crowded lounge to the exit. 'Would you like another cup of coffee, or a brandy, perhaps?'

Obediently, she took another bite from her sandwich. 'No brandy, thank you,' she said, 'but I would like some more coffee.'

'I'll get it.' He fairly leapt to his feet and made for the bar.

Joe glanced after him, grinning. 'You seem to have got him eating out of your hand,' he said.

'You were scared I was going to louse up the whole exercise, weren't you?'

'I was at first, but we managed to get a few things sorted out while you were in the cottage. I pointed out the effect it would have on Leonora's estate if the book wasn't published as planned, and fortunately our "legal eagle" backed me up.'

'Of course, Round is answerable to the beneficiaries, isn't he? Incidentally,' Melissa lowered her voice again after making sure that the gentleman in question was still at the bar, 'have you any idea who they are? I was dying to ask Semple, but it didn't seem quite proper.'

'Huh! Since when has propriety cramped your style?' retorted Joe with a grin. 'It's an interesting point, though. If poor old

Leonora really was murdered and the burglary was a put-up job – as you seem to be suggesting – then it might have been for an inheritance which could be substantial.' He shook his head, frowning. 'I've no idea who her estate goes to, although I presume Round, as her godson, will get something. As far as I know, she had very few relatives and never had much to do with them anyway. She gave a lot to charity while she was alive, so maybe she's left . . .'

'Shh, they're coming back.' The others had reappeared simultaneously from opposite directions, Mr Round bringing Melissa's second cup of coffee.

'Well, that's that,' said Mr Semple. He glanced at his watch. 'I'm not trying to rush anyone, but I do have another appointment shortly. I wonder, Mrs Craig, if you'd be kind enough to drive these gentlemen back to Cheltenham – if you feel up to it, of course?'

'By all means. I'm fine now.'

'Splendid. Remember to call in at my office, by the way. My secretary, Miss Gudgeon, is preparing a form of receipt for you to sign.' He buttoned his overcoat, which he had slipped on before going outside to make his call, and put on his gloves. 'Please excuse me if I hurry off now. No doubt you'll be in touch if you need any advice or information from me.' With a brisk salute, he left them to the remains of their lunch.

When they returned to the office of Rathbone and Semple, Miss Gudgeon, an aloof individual with a disdainful expression, noted the contents of Leonora's shopping bag as Melissa called them out and showed them to Mr Round.

'There you are,' said Melissa as she signed and gave back the formal receipt. 'I'll leave you my card, just in case there are any queries.' She handed it to the woman with a smile that was not returned. 'Perhaps you'd like to have one as well, Mr Round?'

she added, taking another card from her purse. 'You might like to check on progress.'

'Thank you.' He accepted the card, put it into his wallet and took out one of his own. 'Here's mine.'

In the street outside, she said, 'It's been nice meeting you,' and offered him her hand.

He took it and held it for a moment. 'I apologise if I seemed officious. I'm not used to this situation, and Semple does have a way of . . .'

'Exercising his seniority?' Melissa suggested, as he hesitated. He gave a rueful nod. 'You mustn't let him browbeat you. You're the client, after all.'

'That's what Leonora told me when she said she was going to appoint me her executor. She warned me he could be overbearing at times, and I suppose I over-reacted.'

'I wouldn't let it worry you.'

'I won't.' He hesitated a moment before saying, 'I never actually finished any of Leonora's books – between ourselves, I think they're pretty awful – but I suppose I knew her as well as anyone did. I hope you'll feel free to call on me if you need any help. Maybe I . . .' Again, he seemed lost for words.

'Thank you. I might just take you up on that. Can I give you a lift to the station, by the way?'

'No thank you, I've a couple of hours before my train leaves so I think I'll have a look round the art gallery.' He raised a hand in farewell and walked away.

'So you'll do it?' said Joe as they made their way back to the car.

'I'll let you know when I've read the script right through,' said Melissa, determined not to be a pushover.

'It's a cracking plot, though, don't you think?' he persisted.

'It is pretty good.' Not for the world was she prepared to admit that not only was she keen to finish Leonora's story, but

35

that an idea for a plot of her own had come into her head on the drive back to Cheltenham. For some time she had been toying with the idea of pensioning off Nathan Latimer, the doughty sleuth of a dozen or more of her own novels. A character on the lines of the chief protagonist in *Deadly Legacy*, suitably modernised, seemed a promising alternative.

'And you reckon you can do it in the time?' Joe was saying.

'It shouldn't be difficult; I'll let you know in a day or two. When does your train leave?'

He glanced at his watch. 'In half an hour.'

'Good, we've comfortable time.'

'I'm sorry I can't catch a later one. We could have had dinner.'

'It's all right . . . another time, perhaps.'

'I'm taking Paul to the theatre.' Joe's son was in his final year at Oxford. 'He's spending the weekend with me.'

'That's nice.'

'Yes. Did I tell you, Georgina's remarried and gone to live in South Africa?' He turned to look at her with a searching expression in his deep-set eyes. She knew he cared for her more than she had ever allowed him to say, and was sad. For all her teasing, she was very fond of him, but not in the way she knew he wanted.

On the way to the station they hardly spoke. When they arrived, he unlatched the passenger door, made to get out, then turned back and kissed her on the cheek. He smelled clean, a mixture of pine and tweed. 'You'll be in touch then?' he said, and she nodded. He slammed the door and strode away; she watched as he crossed the forecourt and entered the booking hall, but he did not wave or look back. Slowly, she drove home.

She was about to sit down to her evening meal when the telephone rang. The caller was Detective Inspector Holloway from Stowbridge police station.

'Mrs Craig, we received information that you claim to have

found an important piece of evidence at Quarry Cottage?'

'That's right. A length of angle iron, hidden in a well. It had what looked like dried blood and hair stuck to it.'

'Can you describe the exact position of the well?'

'Certainly. It's in the front garden, on the left going in, quite close to the boundary hedge. It's covered by a circular wooden lid.'

There was a pause, during which muffled voices indicated that the detective had his hand over the mouthpiece while speaking to a colleague. Then he said, 'And this length of angle iron was in the well?'

'Yes, a couple of feet down, on a heap of rubble. The well has been filled in.'

'You're absolutely certain of all these details?'

'Of course I am. I'm afraid I picked the thing up without thinking . . . you'll find my prints at one end. But I put it back exactly where I found it.'

'I see. Are you planning to be at home this evening?'

'Yes, why?'

'I'd like to come and see you if it's convenient.'

'There isn't anything more I can tell you.'

'Will about seven o'clock suit you?'

'I suppose so. Inspector, has something happened?'

There was a pause before he said, 'We sent a patrol car to the scene within an hour of receiving the message. The officers found the well as you described it, but there was nothing in it.'

Chapter Six

'What makes you so sure it was angle iron?' said DI Holloway, not for the first time. 'It might have been a length of wood, for example, that you mistook . . . you admit that you were in a state of, er, nervous tension, shall we say?'

With difficulty, Melissa tamped down her rising anger. 'I was not in a state of nervous tension, as you call it, when I made the discovery,' she said. 'It was only when I saw the dried blood and hair and realised what it meant, that I began to feel a bit shaky.'

'Unless the substances you saw can be submitted to forensic tests, we can't say for certain what they were,' he pointed out. 'And since the article you described is no longer in the place where you claim to have seen it . . .'

'Are you suggesting I made all this up?' Melissa interrupted angrily. She did not often take a dislike to anyone on sight, but there was something about this sandy-haired young man's habit of narrowing his eyes and raising his brows, as if everything she said was suspect, that aroused her immediate hostility.

'Of course not, Madam,' he responded smoothly, 'but I am suggesting that you could have been mistaken as to the nature of what you found. If, in fact, it was not iron but a piece of wood, the brown substance might have been some kind of fungus.'

'It wasn't wood and the substance wasn't fungus,' Melissa declared stubbornly. 'And what about the hair that was sticking to it?'

'It could have come from a dog.'

'If that's all it was, why would anyone go to the trouble of hiding it, let alone removing it?'

'Children playing, perhaps?'

Melissa was about to declare that she had observed no sign of any children in the vicinity of Leonora's cottage, and that in any case they should all have been in school at the time, but instinct told her it would be futile. DI Holloway had no doubt been instructed by a superior officer to check her story and he was obeying orders, but he had plainly made up his mind that he was wasting his time. She was fuming. Here she was, doing her best to help solve a crime and being treated as an unreliable witness for her pains. Despite the provocation, she kept her temper.

'It's unfortunate, isn't it,' she said coolly, 'that the SOCOS failed to find it?'

A slight flush spread upwards from the inspector's collar and she knew she had scored. 'There's no proof that it was there at the time,' he retorted.

'You're suggesting that the killer, having removed the murder weapon, returned later and deliberately planted it close to the scene of the crime?'

'You are making assumptions for which there is no evidence, Madam,' he said through his teeth. He was plainly becoming rattled.

Melissa pushed home her advantage. 'I'm trying to help you form a theory as to why that piece of angle iron – and I'm a hundred per cent certain that's what it was, no matter what you say – should have been removed from its hiding place.'

'Why hide it at all? Why not remove it at the time?'

'Maybe he couldn't carry it. We don't know exactly what was stolen, do we? Or maybe he was afraid of being caught with it in his possession. No doubt you can think of other possible explanations, being familiar with the workings of the criminal mind.' The flush deepened. Out of the corner of her eye Melissa saw the young WPC who had arrived with him biting her lips to conceal a smile. *That's levelled things up a bit*, she thought gleefully. She had had enough of supercilious young men for one day, even if one of them had climbed down and apologised.

'Perhaps,' she continued, 'he saw us all at the cottage and was afraid a search for a weapon was already being carried out. Maybe it was his first opportunity to come back for it, without the risk of being spotted. When we arrived, he'd have had to get out of sight in a hurry. Maybe he even saw me looking in the well . . .'

At the thought, she experienced once again the chilly sensation that had gripped her as she held in her hand what she was convinced was the murder weapon. Had the killer been lying in wait not far away, looking for a chance to remove it before someone else did? The disused quarry offered plenty of cover and she remembered noticing a public footpath close to the cottage. It would have been easy to remain out of sight. And what if, instead of replacing the weapon, she had decided to take it away? Would he have leapt from his hiding place and grabbed it before handing out the same treatment to her as he had to Leonora?

Meanwhile, DI Holloway was referring to his notebook. 'You say you're quite sure no one else heard you telling your three companions of your discovery?' he said.

'I didn't say I was "quite sure", I said I thought it unlikely. Just as I think it unlikely that anyone could have listened in when Mr Semple was making his call to the police station. He did it from his car for that very reason.'

'Very proper,' said Holloway, smoothly, his equanimity apparently restored.

DI Holloway and WPC Shelley had arrived punctually. The latter was perched on the edge of a chair in Melissa's sitting-room, scribbling in a notebook, while her superior was seated comfortably in an armchair. From the outset, his manner had suggested that he had doubts about Melissa's story. It was now becoming clear what lay behind the line he was taking: his men had failed to go over the place as thoroughly as they should have done and he was covering up for them. It was understandable, but if he was hoping to get her to admit to the possibility of a mistake, he had picked on the wrong person.

'I take it there was no suggestion by any of the gentlemen that you should all return to Quarry Cottage to verify your discovery?'

'No, why should there have been? *They* didn't accuse me of having invented the story.' Melissa was wishing more than ever that she had followed her initial impulse to contact Ken Harris. He would have believed her without question.

'No one's accusing you of inventing anything, Mrs Craig,' said Holloway, 'but the fact is, something you claim to be an important piece of evidence is not where you say it was, and I'm trying to establish how this came about.'

It was getting late, and it had been a trying day. 'Obviously, someone removed it between my leaving the place and your officers getting there,' Melissa said wearily. 'The most likely person to have done that is the killer. Maybe he threw it into the undergrowth somewhere. Shouldn't your men have thought of that and started searching further afield?'

'It was hardly practicable; the light was already fading and in any case we didn't have sufficient men on the spot to carry out a fingertip search,' he said defensively. 'Besides, we're still awaiting the pathologist's detailed report. Until that comes to hand, we don't know the precise cause of the old lady's death. If the head injury was caused by her falling against the stone hearth . . .'

'That would make things nice and simple, wouldn't it?'

Holloway frowned, evidently suspecting that the remark was intended as a jibe, but he made no response. He glanced at the clock on the mantelpiece and stood up, motioning to the policewoman to do the same. 'Thank you for your help, and I apologise for taking up so much of your time,' he said, as if repeating a formula.

Melissa showed them to the door and was about to close it behind them when a thought struck her. 'Just a minute, Inspector,' she said. 'You told me when you telephoned that your men went to Quarry Cottage within an hour of receiving Mr Semple's message. Now you're saying it was too dark to make a proper search.'

'That's right.'

'So what time would that have been?'

'Julie?' He turned to his colleague, who was already pulling out her notebook.

She riffled through the pages and said, 'Message received at three-fifteen this afternoon and passed immediately to Assistant Superintendent Bailey. Sergeant Hand and WPC Wright instructed to attend scene of reported find; checked in at four-o-five to say no trace of alleged weapon in well. Brief search in immediate vicinity called off because of fading light.'

'The sun sets early at this time of year,' Holloway pointed out with a hint of condescension in his manner.

'I'm well aware of that,' Melissa said impatiently.

'So what's the problem?'

'There must be a mistake. I can't tell you the time to the minute, but it was certainly not long after two o'clock when Mr Semple made his call to the station.'

Holloway looked disconcerted and Melissa tried not to feel smug at having wrong-footed him. 'You're certain of this?' he said.

'Quite certain. Mr Semple went off to see a client and I drove Mr Round and my agent back to Cheltenham a short time later. I noticed as we left the pub car park that the time was nearly half-past two.'

'Perhaps your clock was an hour slow.'

'It couldn't have been, or Mr Martin would have missed the three fifty-five train to London. We called in at Mr Semple's office because I had to sign a paper and we still reached the station in plenty of time.'

'I see.' Holloway took the notebook and gave it a brief glance before returning it with the curt command, 'Check that the minute we get back, Julie.'

'Sir.'

When they had gone, Melissa went to her study with the intention of beginning a detailed study of the script of Leonora Jewell's unfinished last novel. She was in a thoroughly ill humour after Holloway's visit and began to wish she had never become involved. If Joe Martin hadn't leaned on her to undertake the task of writing the final chapters, she would never have gone to Quarry Cottage, never have found the blood-stained weapon (why did she have to go poking her nose into things that were none of her business?) and would be in the happy position of being able to relax and enjoy a few weeks of idleness. Instead, she seemed to be faced with nothing but hassle. Despite her earlier enthusiasm, she seriously considered phoning Joe in the morning to say she was backing out.

Things were shortly to get worse. No sooner had she unloaded the files and books from Leonora's shopping bag and taken the first half of the script from its folder than the telephone rang yet again.

'Melissa? Bruce Ingram here. Remember me?'

'Of course I do.' How could she ever forget the idealistic young journalist under whose influence she had become embroiled in – and very nearly lost her life over – the Gregory Francis* affair? 'You joined the Bill, didn't you?'

'Yeah, and then I quit. All I ever seemed to do was arrest drunks and shoplifters and sort out domestic squabbles.'

'And you wanted to change the world overnight?'

'Not exactly, but . . . anyway, I'm back with my first love, investigative journalism.'

'I hope you're not sussing out prurient details of politicians' private lives for some sleazy tabloid.'

'Certainly not.' He sounded hurt. 'Did you really think I'd stoop to that?'

'No, of course not – only teasing. As a matter of fact, I saw one of your pieces in the *Gazette* the other day. Something about iffy decisions in the planning department.'

He chuckled. 'That's right. After what I dug up, heads are going to roll in the council chamber.'

'You be careful someone doesn't go after yours – with a blunt instrument. Some of these people have nasty pals.'

'Tell me about it. One thing I learned from my time in the Force was how to take care of myself.'

'Anyway, to what do I owe this pleasure?'

'Actually, I wanted to consult your friend Iris Ash.'

'You want her number? It's . . .'

'Hang on a minute. I seem to remember I wasn't her favourite

* See *A Little Gentle Sleuthing*

person over that little matter of the erring cleric in your village.'

'That was ages ago. Iris isn't one to bear a grudge.'

'Just the same, would you be a dear and sound her out for me?'

'What do you want from her?'

'I want to know if she can tell me anything about the Asser Foundation.'

'What on earth is that?'

'Abraham Asser is a multi-millionaire and something of a philanthropist. Does a lot to promote talented young artists. Is also into "green" causes. A year or so ago he founded an organisation called Art for the Earth's Resources. The game is to invite artists, especially well-known ones, to donate items to raise funds for environmental projects. The works are put on show in a gallery for the general public to see and eventually sold in aid of the cause.'

'Sounds very praiseworthy – provided the proceeds aren't swallowed up in the overheads.'

'Or siphoned off into private accounts by certain members of the administration.'

'Ah! You think you're on to something?'

'No one – not even the artist who donated the work – is ever told who purchased it or what it fetched, so there's no means of verifying the price. The official reason is to protect the new owner from being targeted by art thieves. Some of the works are said to be quite valuable.'

'And you suspect there may be a difference between what the buyer is supposed to have paid and what actually goes into the foundation's coffers?'

'Got it in one.'

'I take it you want me to ask Iris if she knows anyone who's contributed.'

'I'd like to come and interview her, if she'll agree.'

'And you reckon I'm more likely to be able to talk her into it than you are?'

'Something like that.'

'All right, next time I see her I'll mention it.'

'Bless you! I'll call back in a day or two.' The sound of a kiss came over the wire. Cheeky young monkey, she thought as she put down the phone and made one more effort to get down to work.

It was not to be. Within minutes, Ken Harris rang.

'I thought you'd be interested to know we've just had the full PM report on Leonora Jewell,' he said.

'Don't tell me, let me guess. She died from a blow on the head with a sharp-edged weapon such as a piece of angle iron.'

'How the hell did you know that?'

'I've recently developed psychic powers.'

'Be serious, Mel.'

'Do I take it you haven't heard about my phantom discovery?'

'What do you mean, "phantom discovery"?'

'Or how, according to young Hollowhead, I'm incapable of distinguishing between wood and metal?'

'If you mean DI Holloway, we haven't spoken since this morning. What's all this about?'

With what she considered commendable restraint, Melissa gave him the substance of the interviews, finishing with the discrepancy over times.

Predictably, Harris was annoyed. 'Why didn't you get straight on to me?' he demanded.

'I was going to, but with the solicitor and executor there . . . you know how touchy these people can be over protocol.'

'That's putting it mildly. Pain in the arse is nearer the mark.' He sighed. 'Okay, Mel, it wasn't your fault. There's nothing more we can do till tomorrow. It's frustrating to think how much time was wasted. It's not like Des Holloway to make that sort of cock-up.'

'If you say so. I take it you're still at the nick?'

'I'm just off to get something to eat and then I'm going home, unless . . .'

Anticipating the unspoken question, she said, 'I can do you some eggs and bacon and things.'

'Be with you in twenty minutes.'

Well, that was that. Work on Leonora's novel would have to wait until tomorrow. Not that she minded; there were far more enjoyable ways of passing an evening, and spending it in Ken Harris's company was currently top of the list. Humming a cheerful tune, Melissa put the first half of the script back in its folder, switched off her study light and went downstairs.

As she had anticipated, Ken Harris was decidedly not pleased by her decision – already reached, although not yet communicated to Joe Martin – to write the three final chapters of *Deadly Legacy*. She deferred breaking the news until he was tucking into the supper she had cooked for him. He made no comment until he had finished eating, but she sensed his annoyance.

'A couple of months' work! You promised you were going to take some time off,' he grumbled as he put down his knife and fork. 'I'm due for leave shortly and I thought we could go away for a few days.' He got up, relieved her of the kettle she was about to fill for coffee and took her in his arms. 'How about Christmas in a seventeenth century hotel?' he murmured, his mouth moving against hers. 'A suite with a four-poster bed and all the trimmings . . . think about it. We'd have a wonderful time.' Very purposefully, he set about giving her a preview of what he had in mind.

After a while, he said, 'So, what about it?'

'Not Christmas. I promised Iris I'd spend it here . . .'

'New Year, then? Hogmanay in Scotland . . .'

She snuggled against him. 'It sounds heavenly. There is one problem, though.' His embrace loosened and he held her at arm's length. She looked up at him with a straight face, noting with inward glee the blend of doubt and anxiety clouding his expression. 'It's several weeks to New Year,' she pointed out demurely. 'Of course, Hawthorn Cottage doesn't have a four-poster, but . . .'

'Ah!' His face cleared and he drew her close once more. 'Point taken,' he said.

Chapter Seven

The next day was Saturday. Over the entire weekend and throughout Monday and Tuesday, Melissa worked from dawn to dusk – thankfully without interruption – on her preparatory study of *Deadly Legacy*. Towards the end of Tuesday afternoon she received three telephone calls in quick succession.

The first was from Joe. 'How's it going?' he asked, without preamble.

'You were right, it's a cracking plot,' she replied.

'Knew you'd like it.' He sounded smugly confident. 'D'you think you can meet the mid-January deadline?'

'I think so.' She had been about to prevaricate, but it seemed pointless. He would know that if she had been going to turn the job down she would have called to say so before now.

'Good girl!' Relief and a hint of triumph surged along the wire. 'Have you got everything you need? I can put you in touch with Leonora's editor if that'll help.'

'Maybe later on. I've only read half the script so far. I'm making detailed notes as I go along.'

'Her writing's a bit different from Mel Craig's "crisp, dry style", isn't it?' he said with a chuckle, quoting from a recent review of one of her books. 'You can unloose all those adjectives and adverbs you've kept chained up for so long.'

'Oh, I've been guilty of the odd bit of purple prose on occasions, as you well know. Not on the same scale as

Leonora, though. It'll be quite a challenge.'

'Good luck. I'll leave you in peace for now,' he said, and rang off.

Her next caller was DCI Harris. 'It's me, don't hang up,' he said.

'Ken, I thought I told you . . .'

'I just wanted to check you're okay . . .'

'Of course I'm okay. Just frantically busy.'

' . . . and to say I'll be out of town for a few days.'

'Where are you going?' She felt put out, then told herself it was unreasonable to tell a man she had no time to see him and then expect him to stay within reach just in case she needed him. 'Will you be away long?'

'Till the weekend. The Super's sending me to a seminar in Southampton.'

'How very alliterative. Tell me, have you caught Leonora's killer yet?'

'No such luck. The trail, such as it was, has gone completely cold.'

'No one's come forward who saw anything?'

'Nothing of any use. Her cleaning lady went in to tidy up as soon as we took our seal off the cottage, but that was the day before your visit and she hasn't been there since. No one else seems to have been near the place except the postman. We interviewed them both, but . . .'

'It's a pity young Hollowhead didn't get his finger out earlier,' Melissa commented tartly.

'Inspector Holloway is a very experienced officer,' Harris retorted, 'and it so happens . . .'

'Experienced or not, he missed a chance to catch the killer red-handed,' she broke in. It was stupid, but she still felt aggrieved at the put-down she had experienced at the hands of the young detective inspector.

'A pretty slim chance. I think your original guess was probably right – he was hiding somewhere close by, waiting for everyone to leave. Once the coast was clear, it would have taken him less than a minute to nip in and grab the murder weapon – if that's what it was you saw in the well.'

'Oh, come on Ken, what else could it have been? I mean, why bother to retrieve it unless . . .'

'I agree, there isn't much doubt about that, but as I was trying to point out a moment ago, we can't blame Des Holloway.'

'Oh?'

'Semple *didn't* call us until gone three that afternoon. He went to do it, as you said, but found his cellphone battery was flat. He used the payphone in the pub to call his secretary, but decided it was too public to speak to the police from there so he left it until he got back to his office. WPC Shelley went to see him to clear up the discrepancy and said he was most embarrassed and apologetic.'

'I'll bet he was. The thought of admitting a blooper like that in front of young Jonathan Round would have been too much for his professional dignity!' Melissa gave a sympathetic chuckle. 'So, what happens now?'

'We're looking into Leonora's financial affairs in case she had a lot of cash hidden away that someone might have known about, but so far we've drawn a blank there too. She had one current account and never drew out more than she needed to meet everyday expenses, and pretty modest ones at that.'

'What about her will? She must have been worth quite a lot – her books have sold millions of copies in umpteen countries.'

'She gave huge amounts to a dozen or more charities, and she's made provision for them to continue receiving her royalties after her death. Her godson, Jonathan Round, inherits the cottage, but it's not worth much as it stands – needs a fortune spending on it. Apart from small legacies to Mrs Finch – her domestic help – and one or two other people, that's about it. It's bloody frustrating, having so little to go on.' There was a pause before Harris lowered his voice and said, 'Never mind our problems, are you sure you'll be all right while I'm away?'

'Of course.'

'I'll miss you. Maybe you can spare an evening when I get back. Next Saturday, perhaps?'

'Maybe. It depends how I get on with *Deadly Legacy*. If there are too many interruptions . . .'

'Okay, I'll leave you to it. At least, it'll keep you out of mischief.'

'And what's that supposed to mean?'

'While you're busy ghosting for Leonora, you can't be getting involved in any amateur sleuthing.'

'I wouldn't bet on it!'

'Melissa!'

'Sorry, couldn't resist it. Only joking,' she added, sensing official disapproval.

'I should hope so,' he said severely, then added in a softer tone that sent a glow through her system, 'Take care of yourself, Mel. I'll call you when I get back from Southampton.'

'Sure.'

She was still sitting with a dreamy smile on her face, her hand resting on the phone, when it rang for the third time.

'Bruce Ingram here,' said a cheerful voice. 'Any luck with Iris?'

'Oh, Lord!' She had totally forgotten her promise. 'Bruce, I'm sorry, I haven't set eyes on Iris since you rang. I've been working flat out . . . look, I'll call her now, I know she's at home. Why don't you pop round for a drink – say about six? I'll try and persuade her to join us.' The moment the words were out, she wished she hadn't spoken them, but having inadvertently broken her promise to Bruce she felt obliged to make up for it.

In any case, it would be a relief to get away from her desk for an hour.

'I'd like that – thanks,' he was saying. 'See you later.'

Melissa pushed the phone away and stood up, flexing her cramped muscles. This would not do. She must pace herself, go back to her normal routine of starting work early in the morning and taking a break after a few hours. She put away the first half of *Deadly Legacy* and then, more to assess the quantity of reading involved than with the intention of doing further work that day, reached for the second half. As she drew the script from its folder, something fell to the floor. She stooped and picked up a paper-covered exercise book bearing a type-written label with 'Research Notes' printed on it.

'That looks interesting,' she said to herself. 'Must have a read of that presently.'

Iris had agreed, somewhat grumpily, to be interviewed on the subject of the Asser Foundation, about which she at first claimed to know very little. However, under the twin influences of a glass of cream sherry and Bruce's winning manner, she turned out to have considerable knowledge of the history of both the Foundation and Abraham Asser himself.

'Great collector,' she said. 'Quite old now, of course. Very generous to my college years ago. Others too, no doubt. Donated prizes. Once opened his private collection for us.'

'Was this when you were a student? Did you actually meet him?' asked Bruce eagerly.

'Yes . . . no,' replied Iris. 'Saw him once. Endowed a new wing. Came to declare it officially open.' Her eyes twinkled. 'Been operational for half a term, but we had to pretend we'd never set foot in it.'

'That's fascinating.' Bruce was scribbling in his notebook. 'Is there anything else you can tell me about him? When did he set up this Art for the Earth's Resources scheme?'

Iris shrugged and drained her sherry glass. Melissa quietly topped it up again. 'Can't be sure. Five, six years ago. Bought a place near Gloucester. Can't recall the name.'

'Blackwater Hall,' said Bruce, referring to his notes. 'A couple of miles off the A417.' Iris acknowledged the information with a twitch of one eyebrow above the rim of her glass. 'Have you been approached for a contribution?'

'Gave them a water-colour a couple of years back. Never heard what became of it. Still there, maybe.'

'I'm sure it was sold very quickly,' Bruce said gallantly, and received a sardonic grunt in reply. 'I assume you were never advised how much it raised?'

Iris shook her head. 'Got a letter of thanks and a free pass to visit the exhibition. Haven't been since. Too busy.'

'Did you take it to Blackwater Hall yourself?'

'Of course. Wanted to look at the place.'

'What were your impressions?'

'Quite favourable. Except the curator. Young know-it-all.' Iris gave a disdainful sniff.

'I don't suppose Abraham Asser would employ an unqualified person to run his show,' said Bruce diplomatically.

Iris shrugged. 'Chap knows his stuff. Just didn't like his style. Why d'you want to know all this?'

'Doesn't it strike you as odd that you've never been advised that your picture was sold, or to whom, or how much it fetched?'

Iris considered, her thin fingers fiddling with one of the tortoiseshell slides that kept her short, mouse-brown hair in some sort of order. Melissa recognised the symptoms; she was getting tired of being questioned.

'Not really,' she said at last. 'Theirs to do as they like with, once I handed it over. Suppose I could find out, if I cared to enquire.' She put down her glass and stood up. 'Must be going. Hope I've been some help. Thanks for the drink, Mel.' As Melissa was letting her out of the front door, she said under her breath, 'What's he after?'

'He thinks there's something shady about "Art for the Earth's Resources",' Melissa whispered back. 'He's planning a great exposé!'

'Wasting his time. Abraham Asser wouldn't touch anything dodgy,' asserted Iris.

'I'm sure you're right,' Melissa agreed. It was not the first mistaken assumption made that afternoon.

After Bruce's departure, Melissa prepared a quick supper for herself and ate it in the kitchen while studying Leonora's notes. They were written in diary form with the first entry dated early in September, and consisted of information systematically extracted from the books Melissa had brought with her from Quarry Cottage.

When she had finished her supper, she returned to her study and began checking the references in detail, a task made easy by Leonora's meticulous system of annotation. All the books had been published at least a hundred years before; there was a scholarly treatise entitled '*NOTORIOUS ART FORGERIES*', a book of Victorian costume, beautifully illustrated with coloured engravings, and two romantic novels by long-forgotten Victorian writers. Melissa found herself increasingly warming to Leonora. The snobbish *literati* might consider her beneath their attention, but she had given pleasure to millions – and no one could say she didn't do her homework.

She wrote fast, too. At the end of several closely-written pages was an entry dated 20th September. 'Today I began writing *Deadly Legacy*.' In a little under two months, the elderly writer had hammered out nearly two hundred thousand words on that antiquated manual typewriter. Melissa shook her head in mingled admiration and amazement.

'Phew!' she said aloud. 'That's some going.' She reached for one of the novels that Joe had brought her and studied the photograph on the back of the dust jacket. She saw a strong face with regular features and bright eyes full of warmth and intelligence, the face of a woman who carried her years with dignity. Without warning, her own eyes filled with tears.

'I'll do my best for you, love,' she whispered. 'I only wish I could get my hands on the brute that attacked you.'

It was getting late and she had been hard at work since dawn. She closed the exercise book, put everything neatly away and went to bed. She fell almost immediately into a deep sleep, but woke with a start, conscious of having had a vivid, disturbing dream. She had been working at her desk, her hands busy at the word processor and her eyes on the screen. The text blurred and re-formed into Leonora's photograph, but instead of looking at the camera, the eyes were directed downwards and sideways, out of the picture, as if focused on something lying on the desk. In her dream Melissa found herself reaching out in the direction of the sitter's gaze, blindly groping because she was unable to take her own eyes from that compelling face. A voice seemed to come from inside her head.

'In there,' it said. 'It's all in there.'

Chapter Eight

Melissa opened her eyes and sat bolt upright. It was still dark; the illuminated figures on the bedroom clock showed a quarter to six. At this time of year she seldom got up before seven, but with the dream voice echoing in her head as clearly as if it had spoken in the room, she found it impossible to go back to sleep. She put on her dressing-gown and slippers, fetched Leonora's notebook from her study and carried it down to the kitchen. Huddled beside the Aga with a mug of tea in one hand and the notebook in the other, she began re-reading the closely written pages in the faint hope of picking up some apparently insignificant detail that might suggest a motive for murder. Could Leonora, perhaps unwittingly, have stumbled on a piece of information which made her a threat to someone . . . someone who had not hesitated to kill rather than risk that knowledge being passed on?

As Melissa read through page after page of book references, each followed by a brief but precise note of its relevance to the plot of *Deadly Legacy*, her enthusiasm began to ebb. There was nothing here that could have any bearing on the author's death. She felt a little foolish at having entertained the notion on the strength of a dream. It was about as rational as putting one's faith in horoscopes.

Her tea had grown cold. As she got up to brew a fresh pot, the notebook slid from her lap. She picked it up and a small white card fell out into her hand. On it was printed in elaborate copperplate lettering:

WATERWAY COLOURINGS
Proprietor: Samuel Deacon
Prints and Original Works of Art
All Artists' Materials
Expert Framing

The address was in Gloucester Docks. Melissa turned the card over; on the back was written, in pencil, an eleven-digit telephone number and the word 'after' in block capitals.

An initial thrill of excitement was swiftly dispelled by cold reason. Leonora had been writing a book in which forged oil paintings played a key rôle. Possibly – Melissa had read only the first half of the story – she had needed technical information about paints and other materials used by artists that she had not found in any of her reference books. Someone like Samuel Deacon would be an obvious person to approach for assistance.

The handwritten telephone number on the back of the card was not the same as the printed one on the face. Perhaps it was the proprietor's home number? Maybe he had been unable to tell her then and there what she wanted to know and had offered to look it up. In Melissa's experience, people were extraordinarily helpful when asked to share their expertise with writers. He might have said something like, 'I'm sorry, I can't tell you off the top of my head, but I've got a book at home that might have the information you want. Tell you what, this is my private number, give me a call later, say after . . .' After when? For some reason, there was no note of the time. It was a strange omission. Leonora had by all accounts been a stickler for detail.

It was gone seven o'clock and the sun would soon be up. Already there were bright outlines round the curtains; Melissa got up and pulled them apart to reveal a clear, frosty morning. A blackbird, alighting with a flick of its tail on the rim of the birdbath, attempted to drink but flew off chattering in disgust after its beak encountered solid ice. Some hot water would soon put that to rights. The tits and greenfinches had emptied the bird feeder of nuts . . . and it was time to think about her own breakfast. Telling herself there was no point in further idle speculation, she hurried upstairs to shower, dress and get on with the day.

By teatime she had reached an episode in the script of *Deadly Legacy* – here her interest in Samuel Deacon's business card was suddenly and sharply rekindled – where an argument was in progress between two art experts about the technique used to restore a suspect canvas. Was it in order to research this point that Leonora had been in touch with Deacon? Another question, far more thought-provoking, quickly followed. Supposing he was involved in a scam similar to the one Leonora had concocted for her novel, and had mistaken her for a private enquiry agent who was using the *persona* of a mystery writer as a cover? Melissa switched her mind back to her one meeting with Leonora Jewell, recalling the direct gaze and brisk, no-nonsense manner. Where a trained detective would have used a more casual approach to avoid arousing suspicion, she would have put her questions in a straightforward way, checked each detail and made careful notes. A person with something to hide might well have feared exposure, panicked . . . committed murder? The more she thought about it, the more Melissa convinced herself that Samuel Deacon should be investigated.

It occurred to her that Iris, a professional artist, might know of him. She slipped on a coat and knocked at the door of Elder Cottage.

'Thought you were hibernating,' Iris remarked. She stood aside for Melissa to enter, looking her up and down with an appraising expression. 'Shouldn't spend so much time indoors. Losing your colour.'

'I know. I've made a resolution to start walking again. Beginning tomorrow morning,' she added hastily, seeing a gleam in Iris's sharp grey eyes. 'It's too late now, it's nearly dark.'

'Tomorrow morning it is.' Iris led the way into the kitchen. 'Want a cuppa?'

'Love one.'

Iris brewed herbal tea and set carob and apricot cookies – one of her specialities, much in demand at social events in the village – on a plate. Binkie, ensconced beside the Aga, sat up, yawned, stretched and stepped daintily out of his basket to demand his share of attention. 'Who's a thirsty boy then?' Iris crooned, crouching down to offer him a saucer of milk. She straightened up and sat opposite Melissa at the table. 'How goes the Leonora Jewell saga?' she asked.

'Not bad at all. A change from her usual style, by all accounts, but there are plenty of dodgy old masters being passed off as genuine. That's what I came to ask you about.'

Iris cocked an eyebrow. 'Thought it was for the pleasure of my company,' she said, pretending to sound huffy.

'That too, naturally.' Melissa took the *WATERWAY COLOURINGS* card from her pocket and pushed it across the table. 'Do you know anything about this outfit?'

Iris scanned the card and shook her head. 'Samuel Deacon . . . never heard of him. Always buy my stuff from Dodson in Stowbridge. Why?'

Melissa explained. Iris frowned and shook her head. 'You

62

think he might be a crook?' she said. 'Suppose it's possible. Ask your pet cop if he's known.'

'I would if he was here, but he's in Southampton for the rest of the week.'

'Ask his oppo then,' Iris suggested, her sly grin an oblique reference to Melissa's indignant account of her interview with DI Holloway.

'Are you kidding? He'd shoot the idea down in flames on principle. No, if it doesn't become clear by the time I've read the whole script, I think I'll go and have a chat with Mr Deacon myself.'

Iris looked uneasy. 'You aren't going to say what it's about? If he is up to no good, he'll suspect you as well and then . . .'

'Don't worry, I'll take plenty of proof that I'm making a *bona fide* enquiry. If he's on the level, he'll talk quite freely; if he seems at all evasive I'll know what to think and contact the fuzz right away.' Her mind made up, Melissa finished her tea and went home, determined to read the rest of *Deadly Legacy* in one sitting, even if it took all night. And tomorrow she would call on Samuel Deacon.

At the period in which Leonora Jewell's last novel was set, Gloucester was a thriving commercial port, linked by canal to Sharpness and the open waters of the Bristol Channel. As ships grew larger and their draught deeper, fewer and fewer could use the narrow waterway; trade dwindled and the handsome Victorian warehouses lining the waterfront became derelict, until people of vision and enterprise began an ambitious programme of restoration. New and practical uses for the buildings and appurtenances were devised, leading to the creation of a busy waterside complex where commerce, history and leisure each had a place.

It was also popular with film-makers for location shots. As

Melissa parked her car, she noticed a cluster of people gathered along the wharf, close to where a tall, square-rigged ship was tied up, its graceful lines reflected in the smooth water. Gulls wheeled and screeched overhead or perched on the spars; men in old-fashioned working clothes stood around in groups or leaned on sacking-covered bales, awaiting instructions. Some of the crowd were wearing Victorian costume; others, in anoraks and jeans, were manipulating equipment or scurrying to and fro among a serpentine tangle of cables; still more were spectators. The latter were an evident source of irritation to a man in a duffel coat and woollen ski cap who was walking up and down haranguing them through a loudhailer. Reluctantly, they shuffled backwards as he passed and then edged stealthily forward again, necks craning, autograph books at the ready, eyes searching eagerly for a glimpse of a star or two.

Melissa studied the plan she had picked up in the information centre and located Samuel Deacon's premises in one of the converted warehouses. Resisting the temptation to watch the filming, she made her way over a pontoon bridge spanning the dock basin and, after several false turns in a maze of passages and small boutiques, found herself outside a Victorian-style frontage beneath a sign reading *WATERWAY COLOURINGS*.

Through the glass door she saw a square, well-lit area with a desk at the back, facing outwards. The walls were hung with pictures; in the far left-hand corner there was an open spiral staircase, while a sign in elegant lettering announced more exhibits on the first and second floors. The business must be doing pretty well, she thought, to occupy so much space.

Two men stood beside the desk, engaged in conversation. One was in his thirties, good-looking, well-groomed and snappily dressed in a grey suit, striped shirt with a white collar and bow tie, and highly polished shoes. The other was older, casually dressed in a black high-necked sweater, corduroy trousers and sandals, with brown hair drawn back from a high forehead into a long pony-tail. While she was trying to decide which was the gallery owner and which the customer, the question was settled by the younger man handing over what looked like a cheque and receiving in return a cylindrical package wrapped in brown paper. After a brief exchange of farewells, he headed for the door just as Melissa was entering; she politely held it open for him and he strode past her without a glance or word of acknowledgement. One of Nature's gentlemen, she said to herself.

'Good morning, Madam,' said the man with the pony-tail. He had a serious, almost solemn expression, but his eyes were candid and not unfriendly.

'Good morning,' she replied. 'Are you Mr Deacon?'

'That's right.'

'My name's Mel Craig, I'm a writer.' He showed no sign of recognition, only – by a slight tilt of the head and a twitch of an eyebrow – a mild curiosity.

'Pleased to meet you, Ms Craig,' he said. 'Do you want to look at some pictures? Feel free to wander round . . .' His voice was mellow, with an attractive huskiness. Despite her pre-formed suspicions, she found herself liking him.

'Actually, I'm here to ask for your help. Another writer who died recently has left an unfinished novel and her publisher has commissioned me to complete it. I don't suppose you've read any of her books – they appeal chiefly to women – but you may have heard of her: Leonora Jewell.'

She had been watching him closely as she spoke; he showed no reaction until she mentioned Leonora's name, when his expression altered from polite interest to one of surprise and concern.

'I remember Miss Jewell – she came to see me not long ago. She wanted some information about restoration techniques.'

Deacon pursed his lips and fiddled with the gold ring in his left ear. 'Dead, you say? Poor lady. She was quite elderly, of course, but she seemed very hale and hearty. What did she die of?'

'She was attacked in her cottage. The police think she disturbed an intruder.'

'How dreadful!' His shocked reaction appeared spontaneous and genuine.

'You didn't read the reports in the press?'

He shook his head. 'I'm afraid I seldom read the newspapers, other than the arts pages.' He thought for a moment, then said, 'You asked for my help. Is it something to do with what Miss Jewell was enquiring about?'

'Yes. I've read the script of *Deadly Legacy* as far as it goes. She left a very detailed plot outline, but it seems that she either intended to introduce a new twist – it's a mystery novel, by the way – or that she made some further notes that I haven't been able to locate.'

Deacon gave Melissa a keen glance from rather prominent eyes the same colour as his hair as he said, 'I assume you already knew before I mentioned it that she came to me?'

'Yes. I found your card slipped into her notebook.' Melissa took it from her handbag and showed it to him. 'Were you able to tell her what she wanted to know?'

'Not personally. As a matter of fact, I referred her to the chap who left just as you arrived, Gerard Hood. He does a bit of restoration work himself, so I understand. I gave the lady his number – I think you'll find it on the back of that card. He's . . . excuse me.' He broke off to answer the telephone, which had been ringing for several seconds. 'Waterway Colourings, Sam Deacon speaking.'

From the tone in which he greeted the caller, it was evidently someone he expected to hear from. He sat down and rummaged with both hands in a drawer in his desk, the receiver clamped between ear and shoulder. He drew out a bulky file and began turning over papers, then said, 'Will you hold on just a minute, Dave?' He put a hand over the mouthpiece and spoke to Melissa. 'Sorry, this'll take a bit of time. I suggest you call Gerard Hood . . . I'm sure he'll be able to help . . . yes, Dave, I'm still here.'

'Oh, just a moment, please,' said Melissa.

'What is it?' He was beginning to sound impatient.

'It's just . . . there's a note here that says "after" but it doesn't mention a time.'

Samuel Deacon looked as if he was trying to smile but couldn't quite manage it. 'Nothing to do with time,' he said and added, with the air of one imparting knowledge which a well-informed person should already possess, 'it's an acronym. It stands for "Art for the Earth's Resources".'

Chapter Nine

The cameramen had begun filming by the time Melissa emerged from the gallery and it took her a while to edge past the crowd of onlookers, who had finally retreated to an acceptable distance. She waited for a few minutes to watch the popular actor who was playing the hero bidding farewell to a doe-eyed waif – better known as the star of a TV shampoo commercial – and leaving her in tears on the quayside as he mounted the gangway. There had, it seemed, already been several takes and from the energetic arm-waving and colourful expressions of the dissatisfaction on the part of an angry-looking individual in a leather coat and dark glasses, there were going to be a great many more. Thanking her stars that she had chosen writing rather than acting as a profession, Melissa regained her car and headed for home. Her thoughts were a jumble and, as she so often did when wrestling with a problem, she spoke aloud to herself as she drove along.

Don't get carried away. It's probably just a coincidence. Bruce Ingram has had one of his famous hunches and convinced himself there's something dodgy about AFTER. Sam Deacon recommended Leonora to approach Gerard Hood for some information she wanted for her novel. Gerard Hood can be contacted by telephone at AFTER. There doesn't have to be a sinister connection. But there might be. What does Gerard Hood do there? Is he the curator, the 'young know-it-all' whose manner upset Iris? Deacon didn't say. Exactly what information did

Leonora want? Never had a chance to ask. Is Deacon on the level? He certainly seems to be. Did Leonora get in touch with Hood? Probably not, since there's no mention of it in her notes. Why not? Maybe she didn't have time. Maybe she was killed before she got around to it. Only one way to find out . . .

By the time she got to this point in her soliloquy, Melissa had reached the outskirts of Upper Benbury. Remembering that there were a few things she needed in the village shop, she parked outside and entered just as Iris, carrying a bulging shopping bag, was emerging. She fixed Melissa with an accusatory stare.

'Thought we were walking this morning,' she grumbled. 'Suppose you've been off sleuthing again.'

'I've been to see Samuel Deacon, yes. Look, I need a few things in the shop and I'm going straight home afterwards. We can walk then and I'll tell you all about it.'

'*Had* my walk, coming the long way round to the shop.'

'You're not planning to carry that lot home? It's too heavy – I'll give you a lift.'

'You take the shopping. See you later.' Iris stalked the few yards to Melissa's car, dumped her load on the passenger seat and slammed the door. 'See you later,' she repeated and set off for home. With a shrug, Melissa turned and entered the shop just as Major Ford, one of the least popular residents of Upper Benbury, came puffing up the road with Sinbad, his overweight King Charles spaniel. Something had evidently happened; his greeting, normally accompanied by an ostentatious raising of the hat and some pretence of a bow, was confined to a breathless, 'Good morning' as he tied the dog's leash to an iron post. He fairly rushed into the shop behind Melissa, exclaiming, 'Ladies! Have you heard the news?'

Mrs Foster, the proprietress, was rebuilding her display of oranges which someone – probably Iris, determined to make sure she was buying sound fruit – had disarranged. Like everyone else in the neighbourhood, she was familiar with Major Ford's habit of treating the smallest ripple on the surface of village life as if it warranted banner headlines, and her round, pink face registered only a mild flicker of interest as she returned to her usual place behind the counter, casting a sidelong glance at Melissa as she passed.

'If it's about Shire Cottage being sold . . .' she began, but the Major made an impatient gesture with his walking stick, narrowly missing the oranges.

'No, no, not Shire Cottage, we all know about that,' he interrupted. 'This is much bigger news. There's been a robbery at Rillingford Manor. Huge amount of stuff stolen. Silverware, paintings, goodness knows what else besides! It was given out on the local news just now. Couldn't wait to let you know. Warn everyone to keep their eyes open.'

Mrs Foster's air of detachment vanished in an instant. 'Well, goodness me! That's the third big house in the county to be burgled lately,' she exclaimed, her pale eyelashes fluttering with excitement. 'Have the police any notion who did it?'

'Oh, er, international gang, no doubt,' said Major Ford, transparently drawing on his fertile imagination from this point onwards. 'Stealing to order for some drugs baron or other, shouldn't wonder. Money-laundering and all that. Thought you should know. Make sure your Old Masters are safely locked up, *haahaahaa*! Well, I must be on my way. Good day to you, ladies!'

'Er, wasn't there something you wanted?' Mrs Foster asked hopefully.

'What? Oh, er, no, just dropped in with the news.'

'I won't get rich serving the likes of him,' sniffed Mrs Foster as the door slammed. 'Still, it is dreadful, all these robberies. You'd think a place like Rillingford Manor would have burglar alarms, wouldn't you?'

'I expect it has. Some of the villains know how to get round them,' said Melissa. She pulled her shopping list from her pocket. 'Now, I want a wholemeal loaf, cheese, half a pound of sausages and some cooking apples.'

'We won't mention these to Miss Ash,' giggled Mrs Foster as she took the sausages from the chiller cabinet. It was her standard joke about Iris's vegetarianism, to which Melissa responded with her customary polite smile. She paid for her purchases and drove home.

When she emerged from the garage with her own and Iris's shopping, the door of Elder Cottage opened and Iris popped her head out. 'Coffee's ready,' she announced, and popped back in again.

'Good, I'm forgiven,' said Melissa to herself as she obeyed the summons.

'Get anything interesting from Deacon?' asked Iris as she dispensed coffee and home-made cookies in her kitchen.

'Before I answer that, will you tell me why you're so grumpy this morning?' countered Melissa. 'We didn't agree a particular time to go walking, as far as I remember.'

Iris grunted, returned the coffee jug to its hotplate and sat down. 'Been lumbered,' she complained.

'What with?'

'Designing scenery for the Benbury Barnstormers' Christmas show. Cheeky lot. Stay home for Christmas to get on with some urgent work and get lumbered!' Iris snatched a cookie, which broke in her grasp and sent a shower of crumbs down the front of her voluminous knitted sweater. She brushed them away with a paint-streaked hand. 'Good mind to tell them I can't do it.'

'Oh, don't be a spoilsport! The Christmas show is great fun – everyone's so keen. I get the job of writing the script, but the scenery has tended to be a bit amateurish up to now, so we thought . . .'

'You knew about this?' A second cookie snapped in half and

narrowly missed landing on the floor. 'Might have warned me.'

'Sorry, it slipped my mind. I've been pretty busy lately.'

'So tell me about Deacon.'

'There isn't much to tell.' Melissa described her visit to the gallery and her subsequent thoughts on the matter.

Iris was unequivocal in her verdict. 'Waste of time!' she affirmed. 'I can help with gen about pigments and materials, if that's what you need.'

Melissa put down her coffee mug and absent-mindedly combed her hair with her fingers. 'That's the trouble,' she said. 'I don't know what I need . . . or rather, what Leonora needed. Common sense tells me that the reference to AFTER is pure coincidence, but the thought that there might be some connection between her enquiries and her death keeps niggling at the back of my mind.'

Iris gave a sigh of exasperation. 'All that young scribbler's fault,' she declared.

'Bruce? What's he got to do with it?'

'Put all this rubbish into your head. Forget it and go back to the bodice-ripper.'

'It's not a bodice-ripper, it's a Victorian mystery novel.'

'Whatever. If you can't figure out what Leonora had in mind, change a few plot details. Who's to know?'

'I suppose. It's odd, though, that there's nothing in her notes about all this.'

'Not worth noting, if nothing came of it.'

'I guess not.' Reluctantly, Melissa got up to leave. 'Thanks for the coffee, Iris. We'll walk tomorrow, okay?'

'Believe it when it happens,' said Iris off-handedly, but the twinkle in her eyes told Melissa that she had got over her pique.

'Oh, by the way, I almost forgot. Rillingford Manor's been turned over.' Melissa repeated the substance of Major Ford's message. 'Dudley made it sound like a robbery at the National

Gallery, but you know how he exaggerates.'

'The Vowdens have quite a collection,' said Iris. 'Several Impressionists – saw them when I did a painting of the manor.'

'Maybe Dudley's guess wasn't that far off the mark, then. Maybe someone *is* stealing works of art to order.'

Chapter Ten

Mrs Gloria Parkin, the ebullient and garrulous mother of three whose zeal and efficiency made her much in demand as a domestic help in the twin villages of Upper and Lower Benbury, normally 'did' for Melissa on Wednesday mornings. This week, because of a rehearsal of the school Nativity Play in which her children were taking part and for which she had volunteered to help with the costumes, she had arranged to come on Thursday afternoon. She arrived just as Melissa was finishing her lunch, her moon face under its halo of blonde curls alight with maternal pride as she described the morning's proceedings.

'Ooh, Mrs Craig, they was so sweet, they little ones,' she rhapsodised. 'My Charlene's the Virgin Mary and Darren's a shepherd. They wanted Wayne for Joseph, but when he found his robe were one of Charlene's old nighties, he backed out! Said he weren't going to wear no girl's things. My Stanley says it shows he's got the right idea – he were tickled pink!' Gloria, blithely impervious to feminism in all its forms, beamed approval at this show of sexism in her first-born and his father.

Melissa felt a twinge of nostalgia as she remembered watching school productions in which her only son Simon, now grown up and living in New York, had reluctantly agreed to take part. 'I think it's very good of you to give up your time when you lead such a busy life,' she said warmly.

'Oh, I enjoys it, 'swhat Mums are for, innit? And guess what,'

– Gloria, having followed Melissa into the kitchen, had shed her outdoor things and was assembling polishes, dusters and other cleaning equipment as she spoke – 'there's been a burglary at the Vowdens' place.'

'Yes, I heard. I was in the shop when Major Ford came in to tell Mrs Foster.'

'Trust him! He spreads things around almost before they happens.' Gloria's mobile features registered acute disappointment at not being the first to break the news. Her appetite for gossip – insatiable, but never malicious – kept all her 'ladies' in touch with the activities, fortunes and misfortunes of their neighbours.

'Loadsa pictures nicked,' she went on with evident relish. 'My Stanley says they be worth thousands. Wonder if the coppers'll get they back.' An idea appeared to strike her and she gave a wheezy giggle which set her ample breasts bouncing and straining inside her close-fitting sweater. 'They could get Arnie Barron to paint a few to fill the spaces,' she gurgled.

'Who's Arnie Barron?'

'Used to be at school with my Stanley and me. Funny chap, never spoke nor played with the other kids nor nothing, just drew pictures. Something wrong with him, they said – can't remember what they called it. Began with or . . . order, ord'nary . . . no, couldn't have been that, he were quite *extr*'or'n'ry!' Another spasm of merriment set the flesh quivering.

'Could it have been autism?' Melissa suggested.

'That's it!' A note of admiration in Gloria's voice and a glow in her toffee-brown eyes greeted this display of erudition. 'Autism,' she repeated. 'Must remember that. Anyway, he went to a special school. Learned to paint proper, so I heard. Won a prize once, got his picture in the paper. Dunno what become of him after that. Doing time, maybe, like his Dad nearly were.'

76

'How d'you mean?'

'Coppers picked him up over some job, but he got away with it.'

'How was that?'

'Coppers couldn't make it stick. The witness what picked him out changed his story.'

'Maybe he didn't do it. People do make mistakes,' Melissa pointed out.

'On purpose, sometimes. If it's worth their while, like.' A huge wink accompanied this assertion.

'You think Arnie's father bribed a witness?'

'That's what were being said by the boys in the trade.'

'What trade's that?'

'Car dealer. Dodgy, not a legit business like my Stanley's.' Melissa hid a smile at this reference to Gloria's husband, whose used car business in Gloucester had, she was certain, sailed fairly close to the wind on occasions. 'Course, no one knows for sure,' Gloria went on. 'My, is that the time? I must get on. Where'd you like me to start?'

'In here if you like. I'll be in the study.'

Back at her desk, Melissa made a serious effort to settle down to the task in hand. She told herself that Iris was right; it would make sense to complete Leonora's book using the existing notes. In fact, since she was already working to a tight schedule, trying to figure out what new twist the author had had in mind and then fitting it into the existing plot would take time she could ill afford. Best stick to Plan A, she decided as she set up her word processor and plunged into the first draft of Chapter Twenty-One of *Deadly Legacy*.

Two hours later, despite having sat down with what she believed to be a clear idea of what she was going to write, she had filled precisely half a page. She leaned back in her chair with a sigh of exasperation, just as Gloria tapped on the door to say it was three o'clock and would there be anything else because the kids would be home from school in twenty minutes. After receiving her money and the usual compliments on the results of her labours, she departed in a bright blue Ford Fiesta, the latest acquisition from her Stanley's stock of high quality, low mileage, used vehicles.

Melissa watched her jerky progress along the uneven track leading to the road with something like envy. Gloria was an undemanding soul who had long since dedicated her life to the welfare of her husband and children. Her needs were simple and basic; her motto, had she been asked to devise one, would probably have been on the lines of, 'If you can't figure out what it means, forget it'.

That might work for Gloria, Melissa thought ruefully, but it doesn't work for me. Whether or not I use it in finishing her story, I shan't rest until I know what information Leonora wanted from Sam Deacon. Did she get in touch with Gerard Hood and did he tell her what she wanted to know? And – most worrying question of all – could either of those individuals have been in any way involved in her death?

Melissa came to a decision. Returning to her study, she picked up the telephone, called the number Deacon had given Leonora and asked to speak to Gerard Hood.

A woman's voice answered, artificially genteel with a slight metallic edge. 'I'm afraid he's out and I'm not expecting him back this afternoon,' it said. 'May I ask who's calling?'

Melissa gave her name and explained the background to her enquiry. 'I'm having some difficulty getting on with the book without this information,' she said. 'If I could come and see Mr Hood, I'm sure he'd be able to help.'

'You're asking for an appointment?' The voice became noticeably chilly.

'If it's convenient. Actually, I was thinking of coming to see the Art for the Earth's Resources exhibition. If I call in tomorrow, will Mr Hood be there?'

'He'll be here in the morning. I think he might be able to spare you a few minutes at around ten-thirty.' Without spelling it out in so many words, the voice made it clear that Mr Hood was a busy man with important commitments – which did not normally include interviews with tiresome women writers.

'Thank you so much,' said Melissa. 'I promise not to take up too much of his time.' She resisted the temptation to say, '*valuable* time' with a sarcastic emphasis. No point in arousing antagonism. What's the matter with me? she asked herself crossly as she replaced the receiver. I'm getting really screwed up over this job – I wish I'd never taken it on.

Her next call was to the *Gloucester Gazette*. She gave her name and enquired if Bruce Ingram was in the office. He was on the line within seconds.

'This is an historic occasion!' he said.

'Why?'

'You've never called me before.'

'That's right. Up to now, it's always been you calling me and twisting my arm to join in your nefarious schemes.'

'My schemes are never nefarious. They're all carried out with the utmost probity.'

'Give or take the odd bending of the rules.'

'Only occasionally, in the cause of justice. So, what can I do for you today?'

'Have you got anywhere with your Asser Foundation enquiry?'

'Haven't had a chance to follow it up yet. My editor sent me off on another assignment and I've only just completed it. Why do you ask?'

'I'm going to Blackwater Hall tomorrow to see the exhibition and have a chat with the curator. I was wondering whether you . . .' She paused, hoping he would rise to the bait, which he did with alacrity.

' . . . would go along with you? I'd be delighted. What time?'

'A very superior-sounding female grudgingly gave me an appointment at ten-thirty.'

'Forgive me if I'm speaking out of turn, but I had the impression that your time was fully occupied elsewhere.'

From her previous contact with him, Melissa recognised the sub-text of the remark: What's prompted this call? Is there a story in it?

'Something's come up,' she said cautiously. 'I'm not sure if it has any bearing on what you were saying about AFTER . . .'

'About what?'

'Art for the Earth's Resources. Abraham Asser's brainchild.'

'Oh, right. So, tell me about it.'

As concisely as possible, Melissa explained her involvement with Leonora Jewell and the series of minor coincidences that had led her to Samuel Deacon's gallery and a possible connection with Gerard Hood of AFTER. She did not, however, mention her discovery of the murder weapon and its subsequent disappearance, being uncertain whether this information had been released to the press. She had a shrewd notion that what she was doing would not meet with police approval; anything that might draw attention to it was to be avoided.

Bruce listened in silence until she had finished. Then he said, 'You're on. Tomorrow at ten, here at my office. I'll drive you out to Blackwater Hall.'

'I'll be there.'

Melissa's immediate thought as she said goodbye and hung up was that, once again, she was ducking out of the promised morning walk with Iris. She went next door to offer excuses and apologies; to her surprise, instead of becoming huffy, Iris expressed an interest in joining the expedition.

'Might as well use the free pass,' she remarked. 'Take it you've no objection?'

'Of course not.'

It was a decision that was to have far-reaching and dangerous consequences.

Chapter Eleven

The Victorian builder of Blackwater Hall had chosen a commanding site on a westward-facing slope of the Cotswold escarpment, with a fine outlook embracing the Severn Vale, the Malvern Hills and the mountains of South Wales. On a clear day, Melissa remarked to Iris as they stood shivering while Bruce locked his car, the view would be magnificent, but on this raw early December morning, with wisps of low cloud clinging to the hilltops and the Gothic tower of Gloucester cathedral barely piercing a blanket of mist rising from the river, the outlook was bleak and uninspiring. It was not yet half-past ten and only a handful of vehicles besides Bruce's scarlet Ford Escort stood in the windswept car park.

'Looks as if we've got it more or less to ourselves,' Bruce remarked as they made their way towards the house. 'I suggest we go in separately, rather than as a group. Melissa has her appointment with Gerard Hood and I imagine Iris, er, Miss Ash . . .'

'Say "Iris" if you like,' that lady interrupted, with unusual graciousness, shooting him a sideways glance from beneath the huge paisley scarf that enveloped her head. In return she received a smile that would have turned the head of a more impressionable female of any age.

'Thank you, Iris. As I was saying . . .'

'We each do our own thing, right?' Iris was striding along

the gravel path leading to the house like a soldier on a route march, arms swinging stiffly at her sides, her long coat flapping around her thin legs. 'Suppose *you* want to nose around on your own?'

'Something like that,' he agreed. 'There's a coffee shop; we could meet there at' – he glanced at his watch – 'about eleven? That gives us a little over half an hour to get some first impressions. By the way, I'm here as a member of the public, nothing to do with the press, okay? See you later.' He went ahead of the two women and bounded up the stone steps towards the entrance.

'Quite the little scoutmaster, your young friend,' remarked Iris as soon as he was out of earshot.

'He's probably planning to track down some susceptible female member of the staff and worm information out of her,' Melissa replied. 'It's amazing how much people will volunteer, given the right approach.'

Iris sniffed. 'All part of the technique. Show an interest in what they do and get a life history in return.' She came to an abrupt halt and craned her head upwards. 'What d'you think of this pile?'

They stood for a few moments studying the elaborate brick and stone façade of the building before Iris grunted, 'Late nineteenth century,' in a dismissive tone, led the way in and marched up to the desk just as Bruce, without glancing in their direction, received his ticket and moved away. 'Life member,' she announced regally, waving a plastic card under the nose of the receptionist. He was a young man whose pale skin and fair hair curling softly round his ears reminded Melissa of the knave of diamonds. On seeing Iris's membership card he gestured towards a visitors' book lying on the counter and opened his mouth to speak, but he got no further than, 'Would you mind signing . . .' before Iris swept past him and vanished through an archway, above which hung a notice reading 'Permanent Exhibition'. He still wore a faintly bemused expression as he took the business card Melissa held out to him.

'I have an appointment to see Mr Hood,' she said. 'Where will I find him?'

The man showed no sign of recognition; evidently, the name 'Mel Craig' meant nothing to him. He picked up a telephone, pressed a button and said, 'There's a lady to see Gerard. Says she has an appointment . . . right.' He replaced the instrument and handed the card back to Melissa. 'Mr Hood's assistant will be down in a moment,' he informed her. 'Will you sign the book, please?'

That'll be the starchy-sounding female I spoke to yesterday, thought Melissa as she complied. She wondered if Bruce would track her down and whether she would respond to his charm.

The entrance hall had oak-panelled walls and a high ceiling with some ornate plasterwork that appeared to have been recently restored. The reception area included a small gift shop offering a selection of artists' materials, books, postcards and souvenirs, all bearing legends proclaiming their environmentally friendly origins. Alongside was a display of photographs and information sheets detailing some of the conservation projects financed by the Asser Foundation. Melissa was idly browsing among this material when someone spoke her name. Turning, she saw a woman with short dark hair, heavily made-up eyes and a thin, unsmiling mouth.

'Ms Craig? I'm Eloise Dampier, Mr Hood's assistant,' she said crisply. 'Follow me, please.' She turned and led the way through a swing door marked 'Private' and up a flight of carpeted stairs. She wore a cream silk blouse and a navy-blue jacket and skirt, all of which had *haute couture* written all over them; her pearl choker and ear-studs were the real thing and her leather pumps looked handmade. Melissa, trailing in her expensively-perfumed wake, was conscious that her own woollen car coat and flat-heeled shoes were neither new nor the height of fashion.

A door on the first landing bore a sign reading 'Director'. The woman opened it without knocking, preceded Melissa into the room and announced, 'Gerard, this is Ms Craig, who telephoned yesterday.'

'Ms Craig! How do you do?' Gerard Hood got up and stretched an arm across his mahogany desk, displaying a snow-white cuff fastened with gold links. Mechanically responding to his greeting as she took the smooth, manicured hand, Melissa noted that he was wearing the same clothes as when she had caught sight of him in Samuel Deacon's gallery, but in contrast to the boorish manner in which he had brushed past her on that occasion, today he was courtesy and cordiality personified.

'Please take a seat,' he said with a glossy smile. He indicated a chair facing him and waited for Melissa to sit down before sinking back into his own. 'I understand from Eloise that you have assumed the mantle of the late Miss Leonora Jewell.' His eyes swung briefly towards his assistant, who was sitting at his side, her head slightly tilted as if posing for a photograph. She responded with a grave nod and a downcast eye.

'I've been commissioned to write the last three chapters of a novel she was working on at the time of her death, yes,' agreed Melissa.

'Such a tragedy. Eloise and I were greatly distressed to read about it.' Hood gave a shake of his carefully-styled blond head and shot a second glance at his assistant, who responded with another solemn nod. 'It was a great shock to us, coming so soon after we had made the lady's acquaintance,' he went on, turning back to Melissa. 'Have the police charged anyone with the attack, do you know?'

'Not that I'm aware of.'

86

'A tragedy,' he repeated, 'and a great loss to the reading public.'

It crossed Melissa's mind to wonder if he had ever read a line of a Leonora Jewell novel. She knew that among the *literati*, such a remark would be greeted with raised brows and condescending smiles. She was, however, not here to discuss the merits of Leonora's work.

'I know what a busy man you are, Mr Hood, and I'll be as brief as I can,' she said briskly. 'There are indications that Miss Jewell had thought of a new twist to her plot. My aim is to stick to her ideas as closely as possible, but I haven't been able to find any notes to show what she had in mind. I came across Samuel Deacon's card and paid him a visit; he told me she'd been to see him and he'd referred her to you because you do some restoration work.'

Hood appeared taken aback at the suggestion. He and Eloise exchanged glances. 'I don't know what gave him that idea,' he said slowly.

'You mean, you were unable to help her?'

'I didn't say that. I was able to give her some information, but unfortunately she found it counter-productive.'

'Why was that?'

'She told me about the new twist, as you call it, to her plot and I explained in turn that what she had in mind was not feasible because certain techniques for detecting forgery had not been developed at the period in question.'

'So it was the detection of forgery she was mainly interested in?'

'That's right.'

'I see.' Melissa thought for a moment before asking, 'Were you able to suggest any alternative to what she had in mind?'

'Not really, because she was already aware of what was generally known at the time. She said she had suddenly had an idea for a dramatic new *dénouement* to her story, which involved a character who had discovered a secret process, in effect, an anticipation of the discovery of X-rays. She had come across a reference to a chemist who was doing some research on similar lines to Röntgen and later claimed to have beaten him to his discovery. Fascinating stuff, but historically inaccurate.' Hood sat back and shook his head with an indulgent smile. 'I'm afraid she had allowed her fancy to run away with her.'

'Are you saying that what she had envisaged wasn't feasible?'

'Oh, it was feasible, I suppose, but as I said, historically inaccurate, and she obviously felt that made it unsuitable for her book.'

'She must have been disappointed.'

Hood shrugged. 'A little, but quite philosophical, I think. All she said was, "Oh well, I'll have to use my original idea", or something to that effect.'

'And that was all?'

He glanced at Eloise with raised eyebrows and she nodded. 'So far as I remember, that was all,' he affirmed.

'She apologised for wasting Gerard's time, and left,' said Eloise. There was an edge to her voice which said, as clearly as words, *'and I suggest you do the same'.*

'Well, that would seem to be that.' Melissa put away her notebook, which she had – with misplaced optimism – kept at the ready throughout the short interview. 'At least, I know what to do now.'

A flicker of something like disquiet passed briefly over Hood's face. 'You mean . . . ?' he asked warily.

'I mean, I shall do as Leonora intended – stick to Plan A, as she called it.'

'I'm sure that's the best thing.' Almost imperceptibly, he relaxed. Melissa stood up and he half rose from his chair. Eloise remained seated.

'Thank you for your time. There's no need to see me out,' Melissa said pointedly. She turned and went to the door, opened it and then thought of something else. She swung round and asked, 'Did you happen to notice if Miss Jewell was taking notes of what you were saying?'

The question appeared to take Gerard Hood by surprise. He hesitated for a moment before replying, 'No, I don't think she did.' He glanced yet again at Eloise, who compressed her lips and shook her head.

'I'm quite certain she didn't,' she affirmed.

'What a pity. She was meticulous about noting the details of her research, so it's surprising there's no record of her visit to you among her papers.'

Eloise shrugged and Gerard, once more at his ease, smiled and spread his hands as if in apology. 'I'm sorry we couldn't be of more help.'

'On the contrary, you've been a great help,' said Melissa.

It was pure chance that had made her turn back to put her last-minute question . . . and to catch Gerard Hood and Eloise Dampier exchanging glances of unmistakable relief.

Chapter Twelve

It was a little after eleven when Melissa rejoined her friends. She found them already settled at a corner table in the coffee shop. The room was crowded; in the half-hour since their arrival, Blackwater Hall had received an influx of visitors who appeared to have made straight for the same venue to fortify themselves with hot drinks and toasted tea-cakes before tackling the exhibition. A background of lively chatter, the rattle of crockery and a tape playing soft classical music meant that the three could talk freely without being overheard.

'How did it go?' Bruce asked Melissa as she sat down and took a sip from her mug of hot chocolate.

'Very interesting indeed,' she replied.

'Did you find out what Leonora was after?'

'No, but I'm pretty certain I found out what she *wasn't* after.'

'Meaning?'

'Meaning that I was fed a load of twaddle.' Briefly, she described the interview, including Hood's version of Leonora's 'new twist' to the plot of *Deadly Legacy*.

'You're sure it was twaddle?' asked Bruce when she had finished.

'Course it was,' Iris interposed. 'Röntgen was a physicist, not a chemist, and he made his discovery more or less by accident.'

'Er, exactly,' said Melissa, who had not spotted this particular flaw in Gerard Hood's story. 'Besides, Sam Deacon said quite specifically that it was restoration techniques that Leonora was interested in. That's why he referred her to Gerard Hood, because – again according to Sam – he does some himself. Hood more or less denied that he does anything of the kind.'

'Wonder what gave Sam the idea,' mused Iris.

No one could suggest an explanation. After a moment, Bruce said, 'So you've no idea what she really wanted to know, Mel, or why Hood concocted that story?'

'Not at the moment, but it occurs to me that she might have had some sort of scam in mind that was too close for comfort to something that pair are up to. If that was the case, they'd have told her politely that it wasn't feasible and shown her the door.'

'You believe they *are* up to something, then?' said Bruce.

'I sense that they are. Apart from his version of Leonora's "new twist", what Hood said was plausible enough, but the body language said something different.'

'Supposing it *was* feasible,' said Bruce slowly, evidently thinking aloud. 'Would the off-chance that Leonora would be unconvinced and decide to use her idea anyway represent a risk to what they're doing?'

'You're not suggesting it would be a motive for murder?'

'No, probably not. The risk of detection would outweigh that of exposure through the plot of a popular novel.'

Melissa sighed and nibbled at her tea-cake. 'If only Leonora had made a note of her visit, or at least what she was after.'

'It would give us something to go on,' said Bruce. He sounded disappointed; plainly, he had expected something better from her.

'I'm sure of one thing,' she countered, slightly nettled by his attitude. 'Both Gerard Hood and his glamorous assistant were relieved when I said I was going to forget about the "new twist" idea and stick with Leonora's original plot. I also got the

92

impression they might be an item. They were constantly exchanging glances.'

Bruce topped up his coffee cup from a white china pot before announcing, with considerable pride, 'I can confirm that. I've had a long chat with Damian, the receptionist. He was *very* forthcoming. I think he fancies me,' he added with a smirk.

Melissa gave him a disapproving stare. 'I hope you didn't lead him on,' she said.

'Well, maybe just a little, to encourage him to talk. He's just broken up with his lover, so he was desperate for sympathy and I gave him some, that's all.'

'I think you're quite unscrupulous,' said Melissa coldly. 'That poor lad . . .'

'Shut up and let's hear what Bruce found out,' said Iris, who evidently did not share Melissa's concern for Damian's feelings.

Melissa glowered at the pair of them over the rim of her mug of chocolate and lapsed into a sulky silence.

'Gerard and Eloise are very much an item,' said Bruce, 'and they're doing nicely, thank you, out of the Asser Foundation. He runs a Porsche, she's got a BMW and they both live it up in a big way. However, as reported to Damian by the lady who takes tea and coffee up to their office, they do have the occasional spat, mostly about his womanising. And that's not all. If a visitor to the exhibition wants to buy a picture, it's not done through the gift shop, it goes through a separate account handled by Eloise. And now and again some wealthy-looking individual, often a foreigner, gets the VIP treatment from Gerard himself; in those cases, none of the staff ever sees which work – if any – has changed hands.'

'It probably happens when there's a very special item on offer,' suggested Melissa. 'An Iris Ash original, for example,' she added, a shade sarcastically. She was still feeling miffed at the pair of them.

'Not necessarily.' Bruce stabbed the air with an index finger for emphasis. 'That's what makes it interesting. Damian's done an art course and knows a bit about values, and he said these characters sometimes turn up to do a deal when there's been nothing special on offer for months.'

'You're suggesting that when someone donates a picture that would command a higher than average price, it's sold under the counter and Gerard and Eloise pocket the takings?'

'It's a strong possibility, don't you think?' There was a short silence. 'What do you say, Iris?'

While Bruce was speaking, Iris had been jabbing a spoon at the discarded herbal teabag lying in her saucer, apparently deep in thought. In response to his question, she said slowly, 'Wouldn't be many private donations of that order.'

'You gave them one of yours. Other well-known artists may do the same.'

'You'd still be talking about hundreds rather than thousands, most of the time.'

'You mean, pounds?'

'Or dollars. Either way, not enough to run a Porsche – or a string of mistresses.'

'So maybe they take a cut from every deal, as well as creaming off the really valuable stuff.' Bruce was obviously reluctant to abandon his theory altogether. 'Damian says they sell a lot of works by local artists, especially during the tourist season. They've even got an "artist in residence" to satisfy the demand.'

'Still only peanuts. Nothing in there,' Iris jerked her mouse-brown head in the approximate direction of the exhibition gallery, 'to raise the kind of money you're thinking of.'

Bruce looked disappointed, but stuck to his guns. 'I'm convinced there's some kind of scam going on, he insisted. 'Melissa thinks so too, don't you, Mel?'

Iris shrugged and said, 'Could be – can't tell,' pushed

back her chair and stood up. 'Think I'll visit the artist in residence.'

'Who is it?'

'Chap I never heard of. Some of his work's on sale. Looks interesting. You coming?' As she spoke, Iris pulled out a coloured leaflet bearing a picture of Blackwater Hall on the front and a plan of the layout on the back. With a thin forefinger she traced a path from the coffee shop before setting off along a series of corridors. Bruce and Melissa followed her in silence until they came to a door on which was painted the word 'Studio'. A sliding panel was set in the 'Open' position and a small framed notice requested visitors to refrain from touching anything and to close the door behind them.

The studio was a conservatory tucked into an angle of the house, so that two of the walls were of brick and the other two, and the roof, of glass. One glass wall looked out on the same panoramic view as that from the front of the building; the other faced north over an ornamental lake beyond which lay an area of lawns, shrubs and trees. Both aspects figured in a number of canvases, evidently by the same hand and painted at different times of the year, which hung around the brick walls. Old-fashioned central-heating pipes kept the temperature at a reasonable level, but after the steamy warmth of the coffee shop the air felt chilly. Melissa drew her coat more closely round her.

A young man whom she judged to be in the mid to late thirties was seated at an easel in the middle of the room. He had a high forehead, a prominent nose, a full, slightly girlish mouth and hair cropped to a half-inch stubble. His eyes, which were a clear, light amber, had an oddly penetrating quality, as if they were looking through rather than at the canvas on which he was working. He had an air of remoteness, showing not a flicker of reaction to the presence of visitors. She had the impression that he was not aware of them, as though his mind dwelt on a different plane where other humans were invisible or non-existent. A ripple of gooseflesh ran down her spine.

After casting a brief glance over the artist's shoulder, Iris marched to the far end of the studio to study the paintings displayed there. Bruce, still subdued after her casual dismissal of his pet theory, remained just inside the door, his arms folded in an ostentatious show of indifference. Melissa ignored him and moved forward to watch the picture taking shape.

It was a view from the front of the house and was already more than half-finished. It showed the landscape menaced by an approaching storm, the distant hills partly obscured in a blur of rain, a layer of mist over the river dispersing under a rising wind. The picture had an energy and movement that was reflected in the artist's deft, confident strokes as he applied paint to a canvas that bore no preparatory sketch.

He had just begun work on a tree in the foreground and Melissa watched, fascinated, as it took shape. It was a tree, and yet not a tree. The gnarled, twisted limbs were sinewy arms ending in twigs like bony fingers; the upper branches were shoulders hunched in weary submission under the wind that raced overhead, tearing the clouds to shreds.

'That's brilliant!' she exclaimed aloud.

The artist appeared for the first time to be aware of her presence. He turned his head to look at her; she noticed that even when his eyes were not on the canvas, his brush did not cease to work, nor did it make a false stroke. He was like a man painting in a trance.

'You like it?' he said.

'Oh, yes!'

'I mustn't give it to you.' His voice had the toneless quality of someone speaking under hypnosis. 'Sorry.' With an air of finality, he turned back to his work.

'I wasn't asking you to give it to me,' said Melissa. 'I was just admiring it.'

'The writing lady liked it and I gave it to her. He got cross. I mustn't do it again.'

'Who's the writing lady?'

'Said she liked the picture. I gave it to her. He got cross.' The words were spoken in the same flat, slightly staccato voice.

'It's all right, I quite understand,' Melissa said soothingly. 'I wouldn't want him to be cross with you.'

There was no further response. 'What happened to the picture?' she asked. 'Did the writing lady give it back?' Still there was no answer. 'Who was cross with you? Was it Gerard?'

The artist leaned back on his stool and contemplated his canvas with half-closed eyes. He reached for some tubes of colour, squeezed a worm of blue paint onto his palette, added one of brown and began to blend the two together with a look of total concentration. Melissa knew instinctively that it was useless to question him further; he had retreated to his inner world where neither she nor her companions had any reality.

'What the hell's he on about?' Bruce muttered in her ear as she turned away, gnawing her lower lip in frustration.

'I'm not sure. I wish I could get him to say more.' Random signals were chasing one another around her brain. In an effort to pull them into some sort of order, she went across to one glass wall and stood staring out at the misty landscape. Supposing the 'writing lady' had been Leonora? Had the strange artist really given her one of his paintings? Was it Gerard whose anger had been aroused by the gift? Why? And where was it now?

Iris called, 'Come and look at this,' and Melissa, glad to be diverted from questions to which she could find no answers, went to join her in front of a garden scene. It had been painted in high summer, with a mass of roses surrounding a statue of

Cupid aiming an arrow at two figures in the middle distance. There was something faintly malicious on the stone face of the god, and his intended victims were looking over their shoulders in an attitude more suggestive of fearful anticipation than a welcome for love's dart.

'Interesting,' said Iris. 'All of them have something of unreality about them . . . underlying menace.' She peered at the signature, almost invisible in one corner. 'Arnie. Good mind to buy one.'

'Arnie?' A bell rang in Melissa's brain. 'I wonder . . . yes, that could explain it. Gloria was telling me yesterday about an autistic boy she knew from school. She said he never spoke, but could draw and paint. His name was Arnie Barron.'

'You reckon it's him?' Iris jerked her head towards the figure at the easel.

'It might be. He's about the right age.'

'He works fast,' Iris commented. 'See how much he's done since we came in? Almost finished.'

The door opened and Eloise Dampier entered, carrying a new canvas on its stretcher. She put it carefully on a table in the corner and went over to speak to the artist.

'Very good, Arnie,' she said. 'That's ready, isn't it? Shall I take it?'

She made a movement as if to remove the picture from the easel, but he put out an arm to protect it.

'Not done yet,' he said urgently. It was the first time he had spoken with any sign of emotion. 'Wait.'

'I think it's lovely, just as it is,' said Eloise. They were coaxing words, but spoken with an undercurrent of steel. 'I've brought you a nice new canvas. I want you to paint a very special picture on it.' She swung round as she spoke, with the evident intention of fetching the blank canvas, just as Iris picked it up and began idly examining it.

'Kindly give that to me!' barked Eloise. 'Didn't you see the notice?'

In an unhurried manner, Iris turned to face her. 'What's your problem?' she asked, with an unusually aggressive expression on her sharp features and making no attempt to relinquish the canvas. 'Only looking. For your information, I'm an artist myself. Merely wondered where you get your supplies.' She was turning it over as she spoke. 'Good quality stuff,' she went on. 'What d'you pay for it?'

'I really have no idea,' snapped Eloise. 'Let me have it, please. We particularly ask visitors not to touch anything.'

With exaggerated care, Iris complied. Then she grabbed Melissa by the arm. 'Let's go,' she said.

'No, wait. Watch what Arnie's doing.'

With rapid strokes he was adding a figure to his composition. It was a woman's figure. A small, slight woman with snow-white hair, wearing a long grey dress and holding an oblong shape in her hands. He sat back and regarded his handiwork with his head on one side.

'Finished now,' he announced.

Melissa drew a sharp breath. 'Arnie, is that the writing lady?' she asked.

He did not appear to have heard the question. With his eyes still on the canvas, he gave a faint, mysterious smile.

'Give me the picture, Arnie,' said Eloise sharply.

'It *is* the writing lady, isn't it?' Melissa persisted, ignoring the woman's impatient gesture.

Slowly, Arnie nodded. 'The writing lady,' he said, almost under his breath. 'She liked the picture so I gave it to her.'

Chapter Thirteen

'What was so special about that canvas, Iris?' asked Bruce as he fastened his seat belt and turned the key in the ignition.

'Who said it was special?' countered Iris. She was making a great to-do about settling herself, her bulky shoulder bag and the thick folds of her coat in the back seat of the Escort while Melissa got in the front.

'You were looking at it pretty closely,' Bruce pointed out.

'Wanted to annoy Eloise.' Melissa, attempting to tidy her windblown hair and peering into the vanity mirror over the front passenger seat as she did so, saw the glint of mischief in her friend's eye and wondered if she was up to something. 'Officious cow,' Iris added genially.

Bruce gave an appreciative chuckle. 'She did get hot under the collar,' he agreed. For a few moments he drove in silence, then said, 'I think I'll see what I can turn up about Arnie. You said Gloria knows his background, Melissa?'

'If he's the Arnie Barron she was telling me about, he was transferred to a special school for autistics. You might be able to check on him that way, but I don't see how it would help.'

'You never know. As Iris says, he has an unusual talent. What do they charge for his pictures, Iris?'

'Didn't ask.'

'I thought you were thinking of buying one.'

'Changed my mind when Eloise cut up rough over the canvas.'

'Whatever his work sells for, it wouldn't surprise me if he only picks up a fraction of it,' said Bruce thoughtfully. 'A chap with his limitations is wide open to exploitation by opportunists like Gerard and Eloise. I'll certainly try to find out a bit more about him. Any idea where the special school is, Melissa?'

'In the Bristol area, I imagine – that's where Gloria hails from. I'll have to ask her.'

'Will you do that? If she wants to know what it's about, tell her I'm researching a feature on *idiots savants*.'

There was a sardonic cackle from the back seat. 'That'd be right over her fluffy head. Have to think of something simpler,' Iris predicted.

'I don't want the real reason to get around,' explained Bruce. 'Didn't you once tell me that she's a blabbermouth, Mel?'

'She enjoys a gossip, yes, but there's no harm in her.' Melissa found herself resenting this pejorative reference to a woman who, to her knowledge, had not a trace of malice in her makeup. *And* she didn't remember giving him permission to use the shortened version of her name.

'I'm not saying there is,' replied Bruce. 'I'm just asking you to be diplomatic.'

'You mean like you, when you were pumping Damian?'

He turned his head and grinned at her, unabashed. 'All part of a journalist's technique.'

'Oh, sure. Anything for a story.' She glanced at his profile as he steered the car through the sweeping, downhill bends of the road leading back to the city. There was a determined set to his chin and a resolute look in his eye that told her his mind was busy sifting possibilities. She knew that look of old; he believed he was on the track of something newsworthy and, like a terrier with a bone, he would worry away at it until he had cracked it open and got at the marrow. Okay, she thought, let him get on with it. Despite certain intriguing questions their visit had raised, she had to face the reality of a fast approaching deadline. Normally, she would have been only too keen to know the answers; as it was, she felt obliged to concentrate on the demanding task she had undertaken.

Her tone must have betrayed her mood. Bruce took his eyes briefly from the road to give her a searching look.

'I thought you were keen to unravel this mystery,' he said. 'You seemed so positive there was something fishy going on – don't tell me you're losing interest.'

Melissa leaned back in her seat and closed her eyes. She felt inexplicably jaded and dispirited. 'I am, I mean, I'm not . . . oh, I don't know what I mean,' she said wearily. 'I wish I'd never got involved . . . and I promised myself a break from work and now I find myself lumbered with an urgent commission that's riddled with complications.'

'Forget the complications. Finish the book as it stands,' advised Iris.

'I intend to.'

'What about the "load of twaddle" you got from Hood, and the picture Arnie says he gave to "the writing lady"?' Bruce persisted. 'How do you suppose that came about?'

'Who knows? Maybe he only imagined it – or perhaps he took a fancy to Leonora and gave her a picture on impulse. She probably pretended to accept it and handed it back later. She must have realised he isn't quite normal. Anyway, it's got nothing to do with the novel, so I'm not interested. I haven't got the *time* to be interested.' With that, Melissa fell silent until they reached the end of their journey.

In the car park behind the offices of the *Gazette*, Bruce pulled up beside Melissa's Golf, got out and opened the doors for the two women to alight.

'Want me to keep you posted?' he asked Melissa.

'If you like,' she said, 'and thanks for the lift.'

'My pleasure.' He gave a gallant little bow and his most bewitching smile. Despite her irritation, she could not help smiling back.

When they reached home, Melissa offered Iris a coffee and sandwich lunch which she declined, saying tersely, 'Another time, thanks. Things to do now.' She had seemed preoccupied during the drive from Gloucester, but Melissa, busy with her own thoughts, had paid little attention. She put her car in the garage and went indoors. Within minutes, the telephone rang.

'Is that Ms Mel Craig?' It was a young woman's voice, nervous and hesitant.

'Speaking. Who's that?'

'It's Carole – Carole Prescot from Rathbone and Semple. You may remember very kindly signing some books for me.' The words came tumbling out in a great hurry; Melissa suspected that she was making an unauthorised call from the office and was fearful of being overheard.

'Of course I remember,' she said reassuringly.

'Ms Craig, I want to ask your advice.'

Melissa rolled her eyes to the ceiling and suppressed a groan. Another amateur crime writer in a tangle over a plot! In the creative writing class which she ran at a local college, she was happy to share her expertise . . . but not out of the blue, and not over the telephone.

'What's the problem?' she asked, trying not to sound discouraging.

'I can't explain now . . . is it possible to meet you?'

'Is it about your writing?' asked Melissa, more gently. The girl sounded really jumpy, almost agitated.

'Oh, no! I'm not a writer. No, it's something . . . I think it might be important, but I'm not sure. I didn't know who to talk to, and I thought you . . .'

'Can't you tell me a little more?' Melissa broke in impatiently. 'I really am very busy.'

'Not on the phone,' Carole insisted. 'You come to Cheltenham quite often, don't you?'

'Yes . . . but like I said, I'm very busy just now. Can't you at least give me some idea of what this is about?'

'N . . . no, I'd much rather not . . .'

'All right,' said Melissa with a sigh. 'Next time I come into town, I'll let you know and we can arrange to meet.'

'Oh, that would be . . .'

In the background a man's voice broke in, 'Carole, I thought I told you those letters were urgent,' and the girl replied, 'I'll do them right away, Mr Semple.' With a hasty, 'Thank you Ms Craig, goodbye,' spoken almost in a whisper, she rang off.

Melissa took her coffee and sandwich upstairs to her study, opened her file on *Deadly Legacy* and re-read the three final chapters of Leonora's plot outline while she ate. She finished her coffee, put down the script, set the empty mug on the window-sill with a thump and exclaimed aloud, 'That's a perfectly sound ending, so what's the problem? Get on with it as it is, Mel Craig!'

She set up her word processor and got to work without delay. She felt revitalised; the adrenalin was pumping round her system and the text leapt on to the screen as her ideas flowed. Suddenly and inexplicably she felt as if Leonora's creative spirit had taken charge of her own and she worked steadily until she was interrupted by a call from Joe Martin, seeking a progress report.

'Fingers crossed, but it's going okay at the moment,' she told him. 'I think I've got the hang of Leonora's style.'

'That's great. When you've drafted a complete chapter, will you let me have a copy for her editor to see?'

'Sure. By the way, Joe, did Leonora ever mention that she might be changing the ending of *Deadly Legacy*?'

'Not to me. Why?'

'I just wondered . . .'

'Mel, if you've got some notion of putting in a new twist, forget it. Time is of the essence, remember?'

'Okay, I only asked.'

'Keep up the good work. I'll be in touch. Bye for now.'

It was time to take a break. She got up from her chair and went to the window, flexing her back and stretching her arms. It was almost four o'clock and the light was rapidly fading. During the past hour or so, the clouds had begun to scatter to give brief glimpses of the sun, which was just about to sink below the crest of the hills on the far side of the valley. Deep shadows were already reaching out towards a flock of sheep on the lower slopes; in half an hour they would be enfolded in darkness. Thinking of the long winter evenings ahead, she decided that, after all, it was not a bad idea to have something fresh to occupy her mind.

With only a short break for a hasty meal, she worked on through the evening; by ten o'clock she had produced a working draft. It would need further re-writing and polishing of course, and no doubt Leonora's editor would hack it around some more when she got her hands on it, but it was a start. Feeling encouraged, she put it away for the night and got ready for bed.

She slept soundly and awoke refreshed, happy to see that, in contrast to yesterday's mist and drizzle, the morning was clear and sunny, with a light breeze. She was just finishing her breakfast coffee and toast when Iris phoned.

'Are we walking this morning?' she demanded.

'Yes, all right.' Unwinding in a hot bath the previous evening, Melissa had resolved, now that she had made a breakthrough, to follow her normal working routine, in which exercise and fresh air played an important part whenever the weather allowed.

Gardening at this time of year was out of the question, so walking it was.

'Say eleven o'clock,' said Iris. After a brief pause, she added, 'Got something to tell you.'

Melissa experienced a momentary stab of foreboding. 'It's not bad news is it?'

'Not bad. Interesting.' Without giving her the chance to ask further questions, Iris put down the phone.

Melissa knew better than to start probing the minute they set out. When Iris had something to say, she said it in her own time. This morning, instead of following her normal habit of commenting on whatever caught her eye – leafless trees outlined against the sky, an unusual cloud formation, the odd sighting of a rabbit, a deer or a pheasant – she strode along in silence for several minutes, hardly lifting her eyes from the path.

At last, she said, 'Been doing a spot of detective work.'

'Detective work? You?' Melissa glanced at her friend in astonishment and caught a cat-that-swallowed-the-canary gleam in her eyes.

'You're not the only sleuth round here,' Iris said loftily. 'Want to hear about it?'

'Of course I do.'

'Remember that prepared canvas?'

'The one Eloise got so ratty about? What . . . ?'

'Something odd about it,' said Iris mysteriously.

'I don't understand. You distinctly told Bruce . . .'

'Didn't want him poking his nose in. Not his line.'

'Anything that smacks of a story is his line. Never mind him, though. What was odd about that canvas?'

'The weave on the top was different from underneath. Looked newer as well.'

'So?'

'Went to see Sam Deacon. Found out he supplies Gerard Hood with materials . . . canvas, paints and so forth.'

'I could have told you that. I saw him there.'

There was a short silence before Iris continued. 'Sam told you Hood restores paintings, right?'

'Yes, but Hood denied it. He said he didn't know what gave Deacon the idea.'

'I can tell you.' Iris looked positively smug. 'He uses mulberry tissue.'

'What's that?'

'A special, very fine paper used by restorers when working on old, fragile paintings. Before taking a canvas off its stretcher, they apply a sheet of mulberry tissue with a special adhesive. It protects the painting while it's being handled. Once the restorer is ready to start work, the tissue's removed with solvent.'

'It sounds like the technique archaeologists use for lifting Roman mosaics,' Melissa remarked. 'I don't see what you're driving at, though.'

'Leonora was asking Sam about mulberry tissue – when the technique was first used, that sort of thing. He didn't know.'

'So he referred her to Gerard Hood, because he uses the stuff.'

'Right. But Hood doesn't do restorations, so what does he want with it?' Iris assumed the expression of one possessed of superior knowledge and playing it for all it was worth.

'I know you're dying to tell me,' said Melissa patiently.

'Think about it,' said Iris. 'He doesn't buy prepared canvas, he buys it by the roll and mounts it on stretchers himself.'

'It's probably cheaper, if he uses a lot. The rate Arnie works . . .'

'Not being very bright, are you? The prepared canvas I picked up felt heavier than I'd have expected . . .'

'And the back looked different!' Melissa exclaimed as she at

108

last tumbled to what Iris was driving at. 'You're suggesting there was another picture underneath!'

'Protected by mulberry tissue.' Iris beamed in triumph. 'Clever, don't you think?'

It was unclear whether Iris's admiration was for whoever had devised the scheme, or herself for detecting it. In any case, that was of secondary importance. 'This could account for all the VIP comings and goings that Damian was telling Bruce about,' Melissa said excitedly, her mind racing ahead. 'Paintings worth thousands, almost certainly stolen, disguised as Arnie Barron originals worth only a few pounds, taken out of the country without a licence, without attracting a second glance . . .'

'Damian, yes. Mustn't forget him,' Iris broke in. 'Had a word with him as well. Very revealing.'

'You went back to Blackwater Hall? When?'

'Yesterday afternoon, after talking to Sam Deacon.'

'What else did you find out?'

They had come to a stile. With one foot on the step, Iris counted off on her gloved fingers. 'Point one. There was a great to-do on the day of Leonora's visit . . .'

'When was that, by the way?'

'The day before her body was found.'

Melissa felt a prickle of foreboding. 'Iris, are you sure?'

'Of course. Her name and the date were in the visitors' book.'

'What was the fuss about?'

'Eloise came rushing out to Damian, asked if he'd seen an elderly woman leave and was she carrying a picture? He hadn't and there was a full-scale alert, Eloise and Gerard charging around looking for her. Seems she'd gone.'

'Taking the picture with her?'

'Right. Point two. I went back to the studio, hoping to get a closer look at that canvas. No chance. Arnie was still painting away like one possessed, but Eloise was there too, pretending to read a book.'

'But really keeping an eye on things,' said Melissa. 'Making sure Arnie wasn't seized with any more disastrous fits of generosity, or in case some other inquisitive visitor started taking too much interest in the canvas.'

'Figures, doesn't it?'

'It certainly does. This explains why Leonora's cottage was burgled. They wanted the picture back, and . . .' Little by little the grim truth was edging into her mind, like a cloud creeping towards the sun.

' . . . and they wouldn't want the police to know what had been taken,' Iris continued. Her expression was bleak; she too was coming to the same conclusion. 'If Leonora had reported it stolen and said how she came by it . . .'

' . . . and the police had started asking awkward questions . . .'

' . . . such as why anyone would make all that fuss about a picture by an unknown artist who turns them out like sausages from a machine . . .'

They stared at one another with a growing sense of horror. The chill that crept over Melissa had nothing to do with the weather. 'Oh Iris, you know what this means, don't you? Leonora didn't die because she happened to disturb an intruder. She was deliberately, cold-bloodedly murdered!'

Chapter Fourteen

By mutual agreement, they turned and headed for home.

'The police should be told about this,' said Melissa as she unlocked her front door. 'I'm going to call Ken – he was due back yesterday evening. Come in with me, Iris. He may want to speak to you.' She kicked off her walking boots, flung her anorak on a chair, hurried to the kitchen phone and tapped out DCI Harris's home number.

'Damn,' she muttered as the answering machine clicked into life and the recorded voice spoke its carefully worded, anonymous message. 'I suppose he's having a lie-in after the seminar.' She waited impatiently for the tone, then said, 'Ken, it's Melissa. Iris and I have some information about a visit Leonora Jewell paid shortly before she died. Please call me back as soon as you can.'

'Going to leave it at that?' Iris looked disappointed.

'What else can we do at the moment? We're not going to talk to Inspector Stuck-up Holloway, if that's what you're thinking,' she added, seeing Iris about to protest. 'He wouldn't take us seriously – he thinks I've got an overheated imagination as it is. There's no desperate urgency, is there? Ken's sure to call back soon.' *He should have called before now; he was due home yesterday*, said a disturbing voice in her head.

'Fresh evidence. Holloway'd have to listen,' protested Iris.

'What evidence?' The word was like a splash of cold water,

dousing the excitement that Iris's observations had aroused. Slowly, Melissa sat down at the table and propped her chin in her hands. 'We've no evidence of any actual wrongdoing.'

'Grounds for suspicion, then.'

'I'm not sure we've even got that. There are just two things we know for certain: that Leonora was at Blackwater the day before her body was found and that she had gone there at Sam Deacon's suggestion to ask Gerard Hood about mulberry tissue. The rest is either hearsay or surmise on our part.'

'Hood lied to you,' Iris pointed out. 'Never mentioned mulberry tissue when you asked what Leonora was after.'

'That's true – and presumably he lied to her as well.' Melissa reflected for a moment, then said, half to herself, 'Suppose he were to be questioned about that, what might he say? That she had hit on a feasible way of disguising old masters for illegal purposes and he didn't think it a good idea for it to be used in a book?'

'Afraid some crook might copy it, you mean?' Iris, seated opposite Melissa and hunched forward over folded arms, considered the point with half-closed eyes.

'If the idea's feasible, he might very well think that. You do think it's feasible, don't you?'

'Sure. Once the covering picture was painted, it'd take a close examination to detect it.'

'And a work by an unknown artist bought by some foreign tourist as a souvenir of a Cotswold holiday isn't going to attract much attention.'

'Exactly.' Iris knotted her brows. 'Abe Asser'll be furious. Pillar of rectitude, that man.'

'I've a feeling it's going to be difficult to convince the police to start an investigation without something more concrete,' said Melissa despondently, 'even though Hood did tell me that cock-and-bull story. He already knew I was finishing Leonora's book, so he wouldn't want me to get hold of the idea. All right, let's give him the benefit of the doubt about that. He couldn't deny using mulberry tissue, though. If he doesn't do restoration, what else might he do with it?'

Iris thought for a moment. 'I suppose, to protect a painting, if you wanted to transport it rolled up instead of in its frame . . .' She spoke grudgingly, as if reluctant to say anything to scupper her original theory. 'Still doesn't explain the hoo-ha about the picture Arnie gave Leonora, or the dodgy canvas Eloise brought in.'

'There's no proof there was anything dodgy about it – it was only your impression . . .'

'An *artist's* impression,' Iris pointed out. 'A *professional* artist's impression,' she added with emphasis, lifting her head to look Melissa full in the face. 'Should count for something.'

'It certainly would, if you could examine the canvas more closely in the presence of a police witness, for example . . .'

'So why hang about? Get the fuzz up there with a search warrant . . .'

'On what grounds? Warrants aren't dished out like freebies in a supermarket.' Melissa pushed back her chair and stood up. 'We need Ken's advice; let's have some lunch while we're waiting for him to call back. I fancy a toasted cheese sandwich.'

She prepared a simple lunch and they ate in the kitchen. She served fruit and made coffee; when they had finished, there was still no call from DCI Harris.

'Maybe the message didn't get recorded,' said Melissa. 'He's been away for several days – the tape's probably full.' She tried again, with the same result as before. 'Waste of time,' she said, putting down the phone.

'Probably out buying you a present,' suggested Iris, with an elfish grin. 'Compensation for a long absence.'

'He was only away three days.' Melissa tried to sound matter-of-fact. She had no intention of revealing her impatience to Iris, who played her own love life very close to her chest, but had no compunction in observing and commenting on Melissa's whenever the opportunity arose. She hastily reverted to the Blackwater affair.

'I wonder what went on between Gerard and Eloise, once they realised Leonora really had gone home with the painting,' she said.

Iris shrugged. 'Had a row, probably. He gave her a rocket for letting it happen. Wonder if anyone overheard?'

'That's a thought. I don't suppose Damian said anything?'

'All he said was, they seemed in a great panic.'

'He didn't say what they did afterwards? Whether either of them went out, or made any phone calls?'

Iris shook her head. 'Never thought to ask,' she admitted. 'Sorry.'

'You couldn't think of everything. It would help, though, if there was something more to tell Ken.'

'The fuss over Arnie giving the picture away – that's fishy, isn't it?'

'Not necessarily. It represented money for the AFTER funds.'

'Not all that much. Fifty, seventy-five pounds, a hundred at most.'

'The amount isn't the point. Gerard Hood is accountable to the Asser Foundation for whatever funds AFTER collects. If Arnie makes a habit of donating his work to anyone who happens to admire it . . .'

'See what you mean. Ah! Just a minute!' Iris jerked her head upright as a new thought struck her. 'Leonora's death was reported in the paper. If they had nothing to hide, and if she had something of theirs, why didn't they claim it?'

'Good point. Let's go back to the moment they realised she'd taken the picture off the premises. I think, in their shoes, I'd have

114

phoned her and pointed out that it was all a mistake, that Arnie wasn't supposed to give his work away, perhaps explained the picture was a special order, and asker her politely to return it.'

'Suppose she refused?'

'Why should she? By all accounts, she was a reasonable sort of person. If she did, of course, they'd have had to think again – offer her another one in exchange, for example. But you see the problem, don't you? We've no *proof* of anything dodgy about that particular canvas. We don't even know that it was in the cottage when it was burgled. If Leonora agreed to hand it back, that'd be the end of it.'

'They'd have to be ready to say what became of it, if they were asked.'

'True. If they invented a fictitious customer, there'd be the risk of a check. That's assuming they were thinking that far ahead . . .' Melissa was putting herself in the mind of a villain with a problem. It was something she did so often for the purposes of her plots that it was almost second nature. 'I think,' she said after a moment, 'the story might have been that Leonora wanted to keep the painting and offered to pay for it. When they read about the burglary, they assumed the painting had been pinched and because it wasn't especially valuable, they'd written it off rather than bother the police with it. That'd be their story, if questions were ever asked.' Increasingly, despite being as sure as Iris that there was something sinister going on, Melissa was beginning to see the weakness of their case. 'You know, there's nothing to suggest that isn't what really happened. Leonora could have been attacked by a burglar who was looking for money for drugs . . .'

'Except for the dodgy canvas,' Iris insisted.

'Ah, yes. The artist's impression,' said Melissa. She made a helpless gesture with her hands. 'It wouldn't stand up in court, I'm afraid.'

Iris sighed. 'Thought I'd cracked it,' she said ruefully.

'You've suggested what might be a very useful lead. I'll tell Ken as soon as he calls back; I expect he'll want to come and see you.'

'He'll want to see *you* first,' said Iris. Her tone, and the sly grin which accompanied the words, could have only one interpretation. 'How long since . . . ?'

'Last Friday.' Melissa felt her cheeks go warm.

'Surprised he wasn't round here the minute he got back.'

'He knows how busy I am at the moment,' said Melissa defensively.

As soon as Iris left, she went up to her study. She had made good progress that morning; the spark of inspiration had been glowing brightly and she was now so involved with Leonora's characters that they were almost as real to her as if she had created them herself. She settled down at the keyboard, determined to push Iris's revelations to the back of her mind until she had a chance to discuss them with Ken Harris.

The weekend passed and there was still no word from him. By Monday morning she was thoroughly uneasy; after trying his home number yet again and receiving the same recorded message, she was tempted to call police headquarters to ask where he was, but held back. They had agreed, once their relationship had moved to an intimate footing, that she would contact him there only in an emergency. 'I don't want some nerd spreading innuendos about us,' he had said after they made love for the first time, and she had replied, 'And I don't want to be thought of as Sir's bit on the side.' She remembered how they had giggled together like a pair of teenagers with a guilty secret, and the ache of anxiety became sharper.

Iris called for her at eleven o'clock and they went for their usual walk. The weather reflected Melissa's mood: dull and cheerless, with a north-easterly air-stream bringing a cold drizzle that threatened to turn to snow.

'No word from Ken?' asked Iris as they set off, muffled to the ears, heads bent against the wind.

'No. I can't understand it. He might be busy, but he could at least find a couple of minutes to return my call.' As she spoke, it dawned on Melissa how unreasonable she was being. Not long ago, their positions had been reversed and when he reproached her she had given him short shrift. Perhaps he was getting his own back. The thought cheered and annoyed her at the same time.

'Probably tied up with the latest "Sex Strangler" case,' suggested Iris.

Melissa looked at her in surprise. 'There's been another attack?'

'You didn't see the report? It was in Saturday night's *Gazette*.'

'I haven't opened a newspaper for several days. Was the victim hurt?'

'Dead.'

'Oh, my God. That's exactly what Ken said they were afraid of. Where did it happen?'

'They don't know where the attack took place. The body was found on Cleeve Common.'

'How dreadful. Ken told me they'd questioned someone after the last incident, but couldn't hold him for lack of evidence. They'll all feel dreadful if it turns out to have been the same man.'

They finished their walk early and in comparative silence, their spirits subdued by a combination of bad weather and the latest tragedy. Back indoors, Melissa watched the local television news programme while she ate her lunch.

As she expected, the main item was the discovery of the trussed-up, half-naked body of a young woman, apparently yet another – and the most unfortunate – victim of the man who had become known as the 'Sex Strangler'. A senior police officer was interviewed, appealing for witnesses and saying, 'This is what we feared would happen. This man *must* be caught', but Melissa hardly heard his statement. One image was freeze-framed on her retina, blotting out everything else: the face of the victim, a young woman who had shyly confessed to being her devoted fan, for whom she had signed several books and who, only three days ago, had telephoned to beg for a meeting so that she could tell her about 'something that might be important'.

The face of Carole Prescot.

Chapter Fifteen

Halfway through tapping out the number of police headquarters, Melissa put the phone down, telling herself it would be better to go there in person to make her statement. She pushed aside the unworthy thought – unworthy because the violent death of a young woman made her anxiety about Ken Harris seem relatively unimportant – that by so doing she might snatch a moment with him. At least, she reasoned as she drove into the visitors' car park, this explained his silence. He must have been working on the case, probably with very little sleep, since returning home.

A young WPC was at the desk, relaying messages between someone at the other end of the telephone she held to her ear and a middle-aged officer standing at her elbow. Melissa had known Sergeant Waters since the early days of her acquaintance with DCI Harris; he caught her eye, gave a friendly salute and, as soon as the conversation ended, came across to speak to her.

'Mrs Craig, good afternoon. I was going to get in touch with you,' he said, in his soft Gloucestershire accent. Behind his smile, his expression was serious.

'Oh, why?'

He glanced round, as if concerned that what he had to say should not be overheard. 'Perhaps you'd like to come through to an interview room,' he said. 'Unless . . . is there something you wanted to report?'

'That's why I'm here. It's about Carole Prescot. Is Chief Inspector Harris . . . ?'

His manner altered slightly, becoming more official. 'You have some information? This way, please.' Without giving her a chance to finish her question, he led her along a passage to a barely furnished room with dingy green walls, motioned her to a chair and closed the door. He sat down opposite her, pulled out his notebook and placed it on the table between them. 'Ready when you are,' he said.

Convinced that his reason for intending to contact her had something to do with Ken Harris, it was all Melissa could do not to question him about it right away. She reminded herself, with another twinge of guilt, that her personal problems were as nothing compared to the brutal murder of Carole Prescot.

During the drive into town, she had mentally gone over her last conversation with the dead girl, anxious not to omit any detail that might help in the hunt for her killer. It was, she realised as she repeated it to Sergeant Waters, pitifully lacking in content.

'And she gave absolutely no indication of what she wanted to talk about?' he asked when she had finished.

'None at all, except she was quite definite it wasn't anything to do with writing. Although,' she added, 'on reflection, that might have been the reason just the same.'

'Why should she lie about it?'

'People are sometimes very reluctant to admit they write. They get embarrassed, afraid of being teased. Maybe she didn't want anyone in the office to know. I got the impression when I met her that she was quite a shy person.'

Waters gave a nod of understanding. 'So she might after all have wanted to talk about writing,' he said thoughtfully. 'In that case, why call from the office and risk being overheard? The phone in the house where she lived has been cut off because the landlord hasn't paid the bill, but she could have used a public call box.'

'Maybe she suddenly plucked up courage and decided to do it there and then.'

'She didn't say it was urgent?'

'No, just that it "might be important" and she "didn't know who else to speak to". When I said I'd meet her next time I was in Cheltenham, she seemed to accept that. Or rather, she didn't press me further because her boss was saying something in the background about urgent letters.'

'Hmm.' Waters ran his fingers through his thinning grey hair. 'I think we'll assume for the moment that it *was* something other than advice about writing. Perhaps her employer or one of her colleagues can help. I'll send an officer round to have a chat with them.' He closed his notebook and returned it to his pocket. 'Thank you very much for taking the trouble to call in with this information,' he said, still in his formal policeman's manner. 'You'll let us know if anything else occurs to you?' He stood up, indicating that the interview was over.

Melissa remained seated. 'Just a moment, you said you were going to get in touch with me,' she reminded him.

'Good Lord yes, I'd quite forgotten. This case is very much on all our minds, as you can imagine.' He sat down again, looking apologetic. 'I take it you haven't heard directly from Chief Inspector Harris recently?'

'No, I haven't.' Something in his manner set alarm bells ringing. 'Why do you ask?'

'He was taken ill last Friday, shortly before he was due to return from Southampton. He collapsed in the hotel and was rushed to hospital for emergency surgery.'

'Oh, my God!' Melissa felt as if a black hole had opened at her feet. 'What's the matter with him? Is he going to be all right?'

'Acute appendicitis. I gather it was a near thing – he was in intensive care for forty-eight hours – but we heard this morning that he's out of danger. I was planning to come and see you, if you hadn't called in.' His rôle had changed from police sergeant to sympathetic friend; he was the one person who knew how close she and his senior officer had become, and they both knew they could rely on his discretion.

Emotion boiled up in Melissa's throat, making it difficult to speak. 'Can you . . . would you . . . what hospital is he in?' she asked jerkily. 'I'd like to get a message to him . . . send him a get-well card or something.' She swallowed hard, struggling not to break down, forcing her lips into a watery smile.

'Of course. I'll give you the phone number as well.' He tore a sheet from the back of his notebook and wrote the information down. As she reached out to take the paper, he laid a comforting hand over hers. 'Try not to worry,' he said gently, 'they assured us he's on the mend.' He was not much older than herself, but his manner was almost fatherly. 'The Chief's a tough old bird. It'd take more than a belly-ache to kill him.'

Melissa nodded, brushing away the tears. 'I know.'

'Can I get you a cup of tea?'

'No thanks. I'll be going home now.'

'I'm sure he'll be in touch with you as soon as he's allowed near a phone.'

'You've been very kind. Thanks.'

Once indoors, she flew to the telephone. The ringing tone seemed to go on for ever before a harassed-sounding receptionist connected her with Ward Eight.

'I'm calling to enquire about Mr Kenneth Harris,' she said when the ward sister came on the line.

'Are you a relative?'

'No, a friend. My name's Melissa Craig.'

'I see. Well, he's comfortable and making good progress. Shall I give him a message?'

'Just say I called . . . and give him my love.'

They were such banal words, conveying nothing of her raw longing to be with him, to take one of his hands in hers and let him know how much she cared. Her first impulse was to run back to the car and drive down to Southampton to see him, but common sense told her she was in no fit state to embark on a round trip of some two hundred miles on unfamiliar roads. Instead, she sought comfort next door.

'Poor chap,' said Iris when Melissa had tearfully blurted out the news. Ever practical in her sympathy, she prepared coffee and spread home-made rolls with herb pâté, saying laconically, 'You look famished. Get that down you.'

'He could so easily have died,' said Melissa, sniffing.

'Not he,' Iris declared. 'Tough as old boots. Taught you something, hasn't it?'

'What?'

'How much he means to you.'

'I've known that for a long time.'

'Watch it, once he comes home.'

'I don't follow.'

'Play it cool. Let him know how you feel and you'll be his live-in nurse before you can look round. Poor, delicate male-creature, no one to look after him.' The mockery in Iris's tone and the sparkle in her eyes were blatant provocation; in spite of her anxiety, Melissa burst out laughing and immediately felt better.

'You hard-hearted thing,' she said, knowing it was untrue. 'You're just winding me up.'

Iris chuckled and poured more coffee. 'Only a friendly warning. By the way, don't suppose you told the Bill about Leonora and the picture?'

Melissa clapped a hand to her forehead. 'I never gave it a thought,' she confessed. 'After what we agreed, I was planning to have an informal word with Ken, but all this has put it clean out of my head.'

'Think we should report it anyway?'

'I suppose so,' Melissa sighed, 'but not now. I've had enough for one day. Why don't you do it? It was your idea.'

Iris shook her head so vigorously that a tortoiseshell comb tucked into her hair flew off and landed on the floor. 'Not me,' she declared as she retrieved it and rammed it back. 'You're the one with all the contacts.'

'All right, I'll have a word with Inspector Holloway tomorrow, but I doubt if he'll take much notice. Now I must get back to work. Thanks for the food . . . and the sympathy.'

'You're welcome.' At the door Iris said, 'You never said why you went to the nick in the first place.'

'No, I didn't did I? It was about Carole Prescot, the girl who was murdered.'

Iris listened with her head cocked on one side as Melissa explained about the phone call she had received from the dead girl. 'Seems odd,' she commented.

'What d'you mean?'

Iris shook her head, frowning. 'Not sure what I mean. Got a funny feeling, that's all.'

Melissa had been back in her own cottage for only a few minutes when Ken Harris telephoned from his hospital bed. At the sound of his voice, a little huskier than usual, she experienced a tidal wave of relief that washed Iris's wise counsel into oblivion. 'Oh Ken, are you all right? I've been so worried about you!' she said shakily.

'I'm delighted to hear it. Who told you about my little drama?'

'Sergeant Waters, when I called in at police headquarters this morning.'

'What were you doing there?'

That had been a mistake. Now he was going to fuss, the last thing a post-operative patient should be doing. 'I had something to report,' she said cautiously.

'What was it?' His voice held a hint of alarm. 'Mel, what's been going on? Have you had a break-in?'

'No, nothing like that. Please don't get excited or your temperature will go up . . .'

'Just tell me what it's all about.'

'Do calm down. I had a phone call that I thought might have something to do with . . . a case I saw reported in the paper.'

'What case?'

'Ken, you shouldn't be thinking about work . . .'

'What case?' His voice became shaky and querulous; sheer physical weakness was increasing his agitation. She began ad libbing in an effort to soothe him.

'A case involving a girl I happened to meet a week or so ago, a girl who's disappeared from her home. Your people are trying to trace her. She rang on Friday and asked to meet me; she's a fan of my books and I think she wanted to talk about writing. I didn't think it would be much help, but I thought I'd better report it just the same.' *Please God, forgive the white lie and don't let him ask too many questions. If he finds out I'm even remotely connected to an attack by the sex strangler, he'll blow his top.*

'Well, if you're sure that's all it was . . .' He began to sound calmer.

'That's all it was, honestly,' she insisted with her fingers crossed. To her relief, he changed the subject.

'How's the book going?'

'Fine. How long do you think you'll be in hospital?'

'I'm not sure. They're talking about moving me to Cheltenham General in a day or two.'

'That's wonderful. I'll come and see you . . . bring you some grapes and a copy of my latest epic.'

'Just bring yourself.' There was a short interval before he said gruffly, 'Love you', and hung up before she could respond. Which was just as well, for she had no idea what her response might have been.

Chapter Sixteen

Despite making a valiant effort to settle to work on *Deadly Legacy*, Melissa found her attention continually wandering. The combined effect of Carole Prescot's death and Ken Harris's illness had thrown her brain into turmoil. At five o'clock she gave up, brewed some tea and contemplated without enthusiasm the solitary hours ahead. It was ironic, she thought, that had Ken Harris been at home with time on his hands and tried to persuade her to leave her desk to spend the evening with him, she would have scolded him for distracting her from her task. As it was, she would have given anything for a few hours of his company. This must be a variation on Murphy's law, she told herself as she rummaged half-heartedly in refrigerator and larder for her evening meal.

There was little of interest on the television so she went to bed early with a book, fell asleep soon after ten o'clock and did not wake until seven, a good hour later than usual. Skipping her early cup of tea, she showered, dressed and had her breakfast while re-reading the pages she had written the previous afternoon. She had known at the time they were no good, but had felt totally blocked; this morning, to her relief, things became clear again. She went to her study and worked like a beaver for three hours.

At eleven, the telephone rang. Her heart skipped as she

grabbed the receiver, hoping it would be Harris, but Bruce Ingram was on the line.

'Hi!' he said. 'I've been digging into a few things.'

'What things?' she asked, trying to conceal her disappointment.

'AFTER things,' he replied, laying stress on the acronym to make sure there was no misunderstanding. 'I've been making enquiries about certain people. You want to hear what I've learned?'

'Of course, go ahead.'

'Not on the phone. This is my story and I'm not risking anyone else muscling in on it. How about meeting me for lunch?'

'I shouldn't be taking any more time off . . .' she began, but he interrupted in his silkiest voice, 'Oh come on, a couple of hours won't hurt, and this is right up your street. You'll kick yourself for not getting in on the action when you read about it in the *Gazette*.'

'What action?' Memories of several hair-raising episodes in her life that had resulted from previous encounters with Bruce sounded a warning. 'If this is one of your wild schemes, count me out.'

'Fear not, gracious lady, it was just a figure of speech.' Soothing syrup oozed along the wire. 'As a valued associate of long standing, I'm offering to share some intriguing information with you. Of course, if you're not interested . . .'

Caution yielded to curiosity. 'I'm interested,' she said. 'It had better be good, that's all.'

'You must judge for yourself. What about it?'

'Okay. Where and what time?'

'There's a new wine bar called Luigi's just opened in Southgate Street. Shall we say twelve-thirty?'

'Okay, I'll be there.' Melissa put down the phone and glanced at the clock. It would take half an hour to drive to Gloucester and find a place to park, which meant she would have to leave in under an hour. There was no point in trying to write any more, but she could at least begin reading over what she had done so far that morning. She had barely finished the first page when the telephone rang again. This time it was Ken Harris.

'Just to let you know I'm still alive,' he said in a voice that sounded stronger and more cheerful than yesterday.

'I'm relieved to hear that,' she replied. 'Any news of the move to Cheltenham?'

'They keep changing their minds. The latest is, not until the stitches come out on Friday.'

'That's only three days away.'

'It feels like three light-years, the rate time passes in this place,' he grumbled. There was an interval, during which she tried unsuccessfully to think of something encouraging that did not sound trite. Then he said, in a lower tone, 'Mel, I meant what I said yesterday.'

'I know.'

'And?'

'Ken, I . . .' How stupid, she thought, for a writer to be lost for words. She knew what he wanted to hear; what she did not know was whether, if she said it, it would be true. She pictured him lying on his sick-bed a hundred miles away, a childless man of fifty whose wife had left him in favour of someone younger and better-looking and who now looked to her for love and companionship. Her eyes misted over with compassion. Not only compassion, surely. They were lovers; there had to be more to their relationship than that.

'Mel, are you still there?' He sounded anxious, in need of reassurance.

'Ken, you know I care about you a lot,' she said. *But not enough to make a long-term commitment*, whispered a voice in her head. 'We'll talk about it when you're home, all right?' she went on as he remained silent.

To her relief, he let it go at that. 'Okay. I'll keep you posted,' he said. 'Have to go now, my money's running out.'

It was several minutes after twelve-thirty when Melissa entered Luigi's Wine Bar. Bruce was already installed at a corner table with a bottle of mineral water and two glasses. He scrambled to his feet and held a chair for her.

'I'm sorry I'm late,' she said as she sat down.

'Don't worry about it.' He gestured at the bottle. 'Shall I pour you some of this, or would you prefer wine?'

'Mineral water's fine, it's what I always drink when I'm driving.'

'What would you like to eat? I'm told the pasta is home-made. Or how about *gnocchi alla Romana*? It's their speciality.'

'No thanks, I hate semolina. I'll have *tagliatelle* in pesto sauce, please.'

'Good choice, I'll join you.'

He's just buttering you up, he really wanted the gnocchi, said the warning voice. It was working overtime today.

'So what are these earth-shaking discoveries you've made?' she asked when the waiter had taken their order.

Bruce planted his folded arms on the table and leaned towards her. 'As I said, I've been checking up on some of the *dramatis personae* at Blackwater Hall. I began with Arnie. Is something wrong?' he asked as she put a hand to her mouth.

'I've just remembered you wanted me to ask Gloria . . . I'm sorry, it slipped my memory.'

'Not to worry, I used one of my contacts to check out the special schools in the Bristol area. By good luck, the one Arnie attended was the second that I tried. I had a long chat with the headmaster, a chap called Edmund Lanyon. Very dedicated, remembers Arnie well. He stayed at the school till he was eighteen and did nothing but paint. Their funds didn't run to oils or canvases, but they kept him happy with cheap watercolours and discarded computer print-out paper.'

'What happened to him after that?'

'He went to live in a hostel for people with learning difficulties, where he simply carried on painting. Nothing could persuade him to try anything else. An art teacher who used to visit the hostel a couple of times a week became interested in him and wanted to teach him to work in oils, but no one was prepared to pay for the materials. The teacher's name was Evelyn Draper.' Bruce paused and lifted an eyebrow. 'Evelyn Draper,' he repeated with emphasis. 'E.D. Does that suggest anything?'

Melissa thought for a moment. 'Eloise Dampier?'

'Clever girl. Take a Brownie point.'

'You know, I always thought that name sounded a bit phoney.'

'Phoney is right. I'll come back to Eloise in a minute.' He broke off as the waiter put plates of steaming pasta in front of them.

Melissa sniffed in appreciation. 'That smells divine.'

'Don't let it get cold.'

While they ate, he carried on with his story. 'Arnie went on living in the hostel for years, painting away, no trouble to anyone – in fact, he still lives there. Evelyn Draper left, saying she'd got a job in London, but a few months ago she showed up again, this time bringing a supply of prepared canvases and some oil paints for Arnie. Seems he took to the new technique like a duck to water, which pleased the lady no end. She told the warden of the hostel that she could sell his work and took the finished canvases away.'

'Didn't Arnie mind?'

'It seems not. Once he's finished a picture, he loses interest and starts another one.'

'Let's see if I can guess what happened next,' said Melissa, laying down her fork. 'Evelyn took Arnie's paintings to Blackwater Hall and showed them to Gerard Hood. She saw a way of making a bit on the side – perhaps she posed as Arnie's agent . . .'

'Good try, but wide of the mark. Evelyn Draper's job in London was with a small firm of fine art dealers. By this time she'd become Eloise Dampier, probably to impress the clients. Some time after she joined – the dates are a bit vague, I'm afraid – there was a little unpleasantness about a missing painting. No charges were ever brought, but the proprietor would very much like a quiet word with one of his former employees, a man called George Harwood. G.H.'

Bruce paused for effect; Melissa met his eye and said, 'Gerard Hood?'

'I've no proof at this stage, but I'd be prepared to bet on it. Anyway, it's an odd coincidence, don't you think, that one Gerard Hood is curator at Blackwater Hall with one Eloise Dampier as his assistant?'

'How in the world did you uncover all this in such a short time?' asked Melissa.

Bruce smirked. 'Contacts – and luck. Edmund Lanyon was very helpful, and so was Celia Patterson.'

'Who is . . . ?'

'Co-warden with husband Conrad at the hostel. Celia never took to Evelyn/Eloise, said she was too full of airs and graces, especially after her spell in London.'

'So what happened next?'

'Eloise turned up at the hostel one day with the news that she'd arranged for Arnie to use a studio at Blackwater Hall, where he could paint all day and every day to his heart's content. They'd provide the materials and sell his paintings to raise money for AFTER. He'd continue to live at the hostel and – here's an

132

interesting titbit – his expenses there would in future be paid by the Asser Foundation.'

'Who'd been paying them up to that point?'

'Arnie's father, Tom Barron – very grudgingly, it seems. He hardly ever came to visit his son, but he made a point of calling in to assure Celia and Conrad that he approved of the new arrangement.'

'Tom Barron,' Melissa mused, recalling Gloria's comments. 'I wonder if he's in on the scam . . . assuming there is a scam. Gloria hinted that he isn't exactly squeaky clean.'

'I can confirm that. I got one of my ex-colleagues in the Force to check him out. No actual form; they questioned him in connection with a country house robbery a few years back, but no charges were ever brought. They reckon his lifestyle is a little more luxurious than his business would seem to support – he runs a second-hand car and car-hire business – but so far they haven't managed to get anything to stick.'

'You're suggesting he's getting a cut from whatever Gerard and Eloise are up to?'

'It looks that way, doesn't it?'

'I suppose.' Melissa lifted a forkful of pasta to her mouth and thought for a moment while chewing it. 'On the face of it, there's nothing illegal about the arrangement, and Arnie's pictures couldn't possibly command enough to make a three-way split worthwhile. You heard what Iris said.'

'Yes, I know.' At this point, Bruce's enthusiasm over what he had discovered seemed to lose its edge. 'That's the missing bit of the jigsaw,' he admitted. 'There *is* something shady going on at Blackwater Hall, I'm sure of it. The lifestyle, the clothes, the cars . . . everything points to it. Oh, one thing more. I had another chat with Damian.'

'More sympathy?'

'On the contrary, felicitations – he and his lover have made it up. As it happens, he was most appreciative of my sensitivity and understanding, said it had helped him get things in perspective.'

'Well done. Your editor should make you the *Gazette*'s agony uncle.'

Bruce's bright blue eyes twinkled at Melissa over the rim of his glass. 'Thanks for the suggestion – I'll put it to her. Damian had several interesting things to say. First, Arnie is normally taken to Blackwater in a car driven by one of his father's employees, but now and again the old man does the chauffeuring. When he does, he parks in Gerard's private garage, which has a direct entrance to the flat – he lives on the premises – and sometimes stays an hour or even longer.'

'Looking after his son's interests?' suggested Melissa. 'Collecting his commission, that sort of thing?'

'You'd think that would be arranged through the office. I haven't met Tom Barron, but from what I hear he isn't the type that snooty Gerard Hood would invite in for a cosy chat.'

'Anything else?'

'The people who clean the gallery look after Gerard's flat as well. There's a room in it that's kept permanently locked, but no one thought anything of it until one of the cleaners went up there on a different day from her usual one and said there was a sound of hammering coming from the locked room. It seems Gerard heard the vacuum cleaner going and came charging out, demanding what the hell she was doing there and practically ordering her out.'

At mention of the word 'hammering', Melissa looked up sharply. For the first time during Bruce's recital, something clicked in her brain. 'What sort of hammering was it?' she asked.

Bruce looked puzzled. 'How d'you mean?'

'Was it bang-bang-bang, as in nailing down floorboards, or a light tap-tap-tap?'

'I've no idea. Does it matter?'

'It might be the missing piece of the jigsaw . . . or one of them. Can you find out?'

'I suppose Damian might know, or maybe I could track down the employee concerned, but won't you tell me what this is about?' He put on his most winsome, appealing expression. 'Fair's fair – I've told you all I know.'

'Which is very interesting, but doesn't amount to anything like evidence of a scam.'

'Melissa, I think you've been holding out on me.'

'Yes, I have,' she admitted. She glanced round; every table in the place was occupied and the noise level made it reasonably certain that nothing they said would be overheard, but she felt suddenly uneasy. The conviction that Iris was right was growing in her mind.

'Look,' she said. 'This could be something much bigger than anything you've suggested so far.' Briefly, she outlined Iris's theory about the use Gerard Hood was making of mulberry tissue and the possible implications concerning Leonora Jewell's death. Bruce's eyes saucered and his mouth pursed into a soundless whistle.

'That's amazing!' he exclaimed, then lowered his voice. 'How do we prove it?'

Melissa shrugged and shook her head. 'You tell me.'

Bruce leaned across the table wearing the eager expression of a terrier that has heard someone say 'Walkies!'

'For starters,' he said, 'we must see what's in that locked room.'

'We?' She stared at him in alarm. 'I thought I made it clear that I didn't want to know about action . . .'

'Come on, you as good as admitted we've no evidence. Why don't we try and get some?' His face lit up in a grin that gave him the look of a schoolboy plotting mischief. 'Think of it – we might find a mulberry sandwich to hand over to the fuzz!'

Melissa put her hands over her ears. 'I'm not listening. Why don't we just tell the police? I tried all weekend to contact Ken Harris, but I heard yesterday he's in hospital, recovering from an operation. Inspector Holloway seems to be handling the investigation into the Quarry Cottage killing, but he and I don't exactly hit it off. I take it you know him?' she added, as Bruce made a face like someone sucking a lemon.

'Do I ever?' he said with a mock groan. 'He's a good enough detective, I suppose, but his pernickety ways get a lot of backs up. I'm not surprised you don't want to talk to him. So, are you game?'

She made a helpless gesture. 'I'm not promising anything. You go ahead by all means if you want to poke around. Find out what sort of hammering Gerard does in his locked room and let me know. Maybe, by then, Ken Harris will be well enough for us to talk to him about it. Thanks for the lunch, Bruce. I must be going.'

'My pleasure.'

Outside, just as they were parting, another thought struck Melissa. 'While you're at it,' she said, 'try and find out the last time Tom Barron called on Gerard Hood.'

Chapter Seventeen

Melissa drove home feeling confident that she had managed to avoid becoming embroiled in what could be a very dodgy enterprise. With luck, it would take Bruce a day or two to track down and question the person who had overheard Gerard Hood at work in the locked room. Today was Tuesday; if she could stall until the weekend, Ken Harris should have been transferred to a local hospital and be well enough to be told of their suspicions. She was confident that he would take them seriously, despite the lack of concrete evidence. Besides, having something stimulating to think about might relieve the tedium of hospital life.

By the time she reached home, however, her confidence in Iris's theory, temporarily reawakened, had once more begun to dwindle. She told herself that even if the sound the cleaner had overheard had been made by Gerard mounting artists' canvas on to stretchers, it did not prove that a stolen picture was being concealed. It was quite possible that he had set up a small workshop in the flat and did other odd jobs there, such as making and repairing frames. It would be natural to keep the room locked to prevent fragile items and materials being disarranged or damaged by a carelessly wielded duster . . . but in that case, why the concealment, why the agitation at being overheard? And supposing, just supposing, that Tom Barron's last visit to Blackwater had been on the same day as their own, would that turn out to be an innocent coincidence as well . . . or could it be part of an ingenious scheme whereby stolen works of art were disappearing into thin air?

Leave it, she told herself firmly as she steered the Golf through the narrow lane that snaked downhill into Upper Benbury. *If Bruce wants to ferret around, let him. It's his job. Get on with yours and stay out of trouble.*

She pulled up outside the village shop, noting with distaste that Sinbad, Major Ford's dog, was tethered outside. Its owner was inside, counting small change into Mrs Foster's palm; when Melissa entered he gave a broad smile of welcome, displaying uneven, nicotine-stained teeth.

'Hah! Mrs Craig, good afternoon! Turning jolly cold, eh! D'you think we're going to have snow?'

'Not according to the forecast,' she replied.

'Huh! Weather forecasts! Load of mumbo-jumbo,' snorted the Major. He gathered up his stick, a string bag containing a carton of milk and a few onions, and the tweed cap that replaced the battered panama he wore from May to September. 'What's the latest about the Rillingford Manor robbery, then?' Faded, slightly bloodshot eyes fixed hopefully on Melissa's. 'Haven't your pals in the Force caught anyone yet?'

'I've really no idea,' she replied. 'I haven't been following it in the paper, I'm afraid.'

He leered and wagged a playful forefinger. 'Official secret, eh? Won't press you, *haahaahaa!*'

He departed and Melissa turned to Mrs Foster with a sigh. 'I wish I could convince him I'm not some kind of Mata Hari who can worm secrets out of police officers,' she complained.

'Ah, that comes of writing all that stuff about crime and criminals,' said Mrs Foster. '*And* having friends in high places, of course,' she added with a flicker of her pink eyelids.

'That's a myth invented by the Major,' Melissa replied firmly, wondering whether it had been a shot at random or whether the all-seeing eyes of Madeleine and Dudley Ford had spotted her in DCI Harris's company. They might have recognised him from an appearance on the local television, being questioned about some crime currently in the news. Deducing from Mrs Foster's knowing smile that she shared the Fords' convictions, Melissa directed the conversation to her grocery needs, stowed her purchases in her shopping bag, paid her bill and went home.

She was waylaid at her front door by Binkie, demanding admittance. Iris had gone to Bristol for a short stay with friends, leaving detailed instructions and a supply of his favourite food. Melissa filled his dish while he wound himself about her legs, purring hysterically, and reflected that it was just as well Iris was out of the way. She would nag her to death if she knew of the lunchtime meeting with Bruce.

Determinedly putting everything out of her head except the task in hand, Melissa spent the rest of the day working on *Deadly Legacy*. She took only a short break for supper, worked until bedtime and fell asleep weary but satisfied. It rained steadily overnight and well into the following morning, but by midday the sky had cleared and, feeling the need for exercise and fresh air, she went for a solitary walk along the valley. When she returned, there was a message on her answering machine.

'It *was* tap-tap-tap and not bang-bang-bang,' said Bruce's voice, 'and there's more. For the latest developments, call back ASAP.'

Melissa re-set the machine and went into the kitchen to prepare a sandwich for her lunch. 'I am *not* going to call back' she informed Binkie, curled up on a blanket beside the Aga. 'He'll only try and drag me into some wild scheme or other.' She put her sandwich, an apple and a cup of coffee on a tray and took them to her study. She had that morning completed the first of the three final chapters of *Deadly Legacy* and she read it over while eating.

'Not bad,' she said to herself when she had reached the last page. 'Not bad at all. We'll see what Joe and Leonora's editor make of it.' She printed off a fair copy, parcelled it up and set off once more to the village to post it. When she returned, there was another message from Bruce.

'I know you're there because you said you'd be working all day. I'll be in the office till four-thirty, waiting for your call.'

It was already a quarter past four, the sun had set and it would soon be dark. She felt jaded after so much concentrated effort and had been thinking of taking a break before settling down to the next chapter, but the prospect of an evening on her own, with both Iris and Ken away, was about as exciting as a deserted railway station on a foggy night. It wouldn't do any harm to hear what Bruce had to say. On the other hand . . .

In a state of indecision, she returned to the study and began tidying her desk, which she had left in some disorder. One of Leonora's books slipped to the floor; when Melissa picked it up, she found herself staring at the portrait of the author on the jacket. It was her imagination, of course, but for a moment she had the impression that there was a hint of reproach in the eyes that gazed back at her.

'Don't look at me like that,' she said aloud. 'I'm busting a gut to finish your book on time.' Almost immediately, as if the dead woman had spoken, the response flashed into her mind: *But you're doing nothing to help find my killer, are you?*

'If you hadn't called back, I'd have come round anyway,' said Bruce as he settled into an armchair and accepted a cup of tea. Against her better judgement, Melissa had responded to his appeal and agreed to his request to bring his latest news in person.

'I'm really on to something, but I need help,' he went on.

'Surely, one of your fellow newshounds . . .'

'I'm not sharing this story with anyone. Besides, knowing you have a personal interest in it . . .'

'What "personal interest"?' she asked warily.

'The "writing lady" that Arnie was on about – the one he said he gave a picture to – Leonora Jewell. The late novelist whose book you're finishing.'

'We don't know for certain it was Leonora.'

'Oh come on, who else would it have been? Arnie gave a picture to Leonora; she took it home, not realising that what she had was a valuable painting in disguise. Damian said that when Gerard and Eloise found out what had happened they ran around like headless chickens. They had to get it back . . . and make sure Leonora didn't report the loss.' Almost word for word, Bruce spelled out the theory that Melissa and Iris had developed over their visit to Blackwater Hall.

When he had finished, Melissa said, 'You really think Gerard killed Leonora?'

'He had a strong enough motive. It wasn't just a single picture that was at stake, although that would have meant a thumping loss. The whole scam was liable to be exposed.'

'I admit it's feasible, but there are other possible explanations for everything we've noticed.' One by one, Melissa pointed them out and Bruce indicated, in a succession of nods, grunts and shakes of the head, that he had considered them all and rejected them.

'I still think we're on the right track,' he insisted, 'and I intend to have a shot at proving it.'

Melissa gave him a suspicious look. 'Now why do I find that statement disturbing?'

'I can't imagine. Is there any more tea in the pot?' His face was a study in guileless innocence as he held out his cup.

She refilled it and sat down. 'Don't stonewall me, Bruce

Ingram. I can tell by the look in your eye that you're up to something, so come clean. You can begin by telling me the amazing new development you've been hinting at.'

'Okay. I paid another visit to Blackwater Hall this morning, just to check with Damian about the hammering noise.'

'Why not do that by phone?'

'You never know who's listening. Besides, I had another reason for going there.'

'Like, casing the place for somewhere to break in?'

'Well, yes, in a manner of speaking,' he admitted after a moment's hesitation.

She had known all along that this was on the cards, why he wanted her help. Her skin began to tingle.

'I've worked out how we can do it,' he went on.

'Don't count too much on the "we",' she interrupted.

'All right. I've figured out how it can be done, but it's a job for two and I know how you enjoy a challenge.'

'I've risen to your challenges before and had some very narrow squeaks.'

'This isn't dangerous, honestly.'

'I'll be the judge of that. Let's hear the story.'

'Right, well, I wandered round the house and did a recce, but it was obviously going to be a tough one. Apart from the fact that there's a sophisticated security system, the place is a rabbit warren and I'd no idea where to find Gerard's flat if I did get in. Then I had an amazing stroke of luck.'

'Well?' said Melissa impatiently, as he paused for effect.

'Like I said, Damian's on cloud nine and he seems to think I've had a hand in smoothing things out, so he's only too happy to tell me everything I want to know in return. Now, listen carefully. Point one, the cleaner confirmed that what she heard was a light tapping sound. She also caught a glimpse of the room when Gerard came storming out and said it looked like a kind of workshop. Point two, the last time Tom Barron brought Arnie to Blackwater in person was on Thursday morning . . .'

'The day after the Rillingford Manor robbery!' exclaimed Melissa.

'Exactly. Point three, Damian overheard Eloise on the phone, booking a table for two at *Le Vieux Manoir* for seven-thirty this evening. There isn't a night watchman, so the place will be empty for at least a couple of hours.'

'What about the burglar alarms? And how do you locate Gerard's flat?'

'That's where the luck comes in. While I was talking to Damian, who should walk in but a representative of the firm that installed the security system. And guess who he was?'

Melissa shook her head. 'You tell me.'

'Jim Plant, a retired PC from Stowbridge nick. Nice, fatherly old boy, took me under his wing for my first few months with the Force. Still as chatty as ever.'

Melissa gaped at him. 'Are you telling me an ex-copper in a position of trust has been showing you how to make an illegal entry?'

Bruce grinned. 'Not intentionally. He's just a natural communicator. Now, let me show you what I picked up while strolling around with him.' He took a notebook from his pocket and began making a sketch. 'This is a plan of the wing where Gerard his has private quarters. He lives on an upper floor, just above where this bit sticks out, making a right angle. His windows overlook the back garden, here and here. I figure this one,' – the pencil made an extra heavy black line – 'is the one we're interested in; in fact, from what Jim said, I'm certain of it.'

'What did Jim say?'

'That's the really interesting bit. There are two independent security systems at Blackwater. One is for the exterior lighting.

Abraham Asser won't allow permanent floodlights to be installed because they consume too much power and are bad for the environment, so he put in detectors that trigger lights when anyone approaches, but no audible alarm. The internal system works in a similar way, but as soon as one of the contacts is broken or any inside movement is detected by the sensors, alarm bells ring and the police are alerted by remote signal. They reckon to be on the spot within ten minutes.'

'And did Jim tell you how to get in and immobilise all this electronic wizardry?' asked Melissa as Bruce stopped to take breath.

'Of course not, but he did point out a weak spot in the armoury. It's here, right below Gerard's windows. At some time, an extra bit was stuck on the building, but it's only a single storey. I've no idea what the original purpose was, but now it's used as a garage and storeroom. The roof is flat and surrounded by a parapet, so anyone climbing up could easily get in through a window.'

'What about the floodlights and the other devices?'

'That's another weak spot. If you approach at this angle,' – the pencil traced a dotted line across the paper – 'you're just out of range of the sensors on either wall. The only points at which the flat is connected to the internal alarm system are the internal front door and a door in the garage leading to it via a private staircase. It seems that when the system was installed – that was before Gerard's time, of course – it was considered adequate.'

'Hasn't Jim pointed this out to Gerard?'

'Not directly. Gerard's function is curator of the collection and administrator of the AFTER funds. Anything to do with the maintenance of the building and grounds is handled from the headquarters of the Asser Foundation. Jim's going to include some recommendations for tightening up the system in his next report.'

'Okay,' said Melissa. 'You've hit on a way to get past the exterior sensors and you've established that the windows to the private quarters aren't alarmed. How do you propose to get on to the roof?'

'Another stroke of luck. A local firm is doing some tree-trimming in the grounds and the men have left their ladders lying on the ground against the wall. They're ours for the taking.'

'I'm surprised Jim doesn't insist they lock them up.'

'I'm sure he would if he knew they were there, but they're covered by black plastic sheeting. I tell you, it'll be a doddle.'

Despite her reservations, Melissa's pulse was racing like an over-revved engine. What Bruce was proposing was hare-brained, possibly dangerous and certainly illegal . . . Ken Harris would have a fit . . . but if there was a chance of picking up just one solid piece of evidence that would help to find Leonora's killer . . .

Bruce was watching her closely, as if trying to read her mind. She drew a deep breath and met the challenge.

'You're on!' she said.

Chapter Eighteen

Bruce had calculated that it would take Gerard and Eloise about twenty minutes to drive to the restaurant.

'If we're in position a little before seven o'clock, we should be able to spot them leaving,' he said. 'Then we'll know it's okay to go in.'

The position he had chosen was in a narrow lane that passed close behind Blackwater Hall. He had evidently reconnoitred it in advance, for he drove slowly but confidently for half a mile to a point where the entrance to a farmyard provided room to turn. He then drove back towards the main road for a short distance, pulled on to the grass verge and cut the engine. It was exactly a quarter to seven.

'It's best to be on the safe side,' he said in reply to Melissa's protest at the prospect of a long wait.

Spread out in the valley to their left, Gloucester sparkled with thousands of variegated lights, turning the heavy cloud that blanketed the sky into an illuminated dome. Blackwater Hall stood to their right, two hundred yards or so away, its outline indistinct at first, then slowly separating from the background of wooded slopes as their eyes adjusted to the darkness. Two pinpoints of light on an upper floor shone out, flickering from time to time as the wind disturbed the branches of intervening trees.

'Those'll be in Gerard's flat,' said Bruce. 'When they go out, watch for headlights. We should see them clearly when they leave; the garage faces this way.'

Melissa huddled into her thick anorak and thrust her hands into her pockets. With the engine switched off, the temperature in the car was falling rapidly. 'I hope they don't hang about,' she grumbled. 'We'll soon be frozen.'

Bruce gave an ironic laugh. 'They won't. Damian says Gerard gives everyone a hard time if he's kept waiting for anything or anybody, Eloise included.'

They remained silent for a while, their eyes fixed on the two wavering points of light. Then Melissa said, 'I take it you haven't heard whether the police are any nearer finding Leonora's killer?'

'Not really,' said Bruce. 'House to house calls and appeals for witnesses haven't turned up anything useful. With luck, we can give them a new line to follow – won't that be great?'

'Great.' Sitting there in the chilly darkness, Melissa felt her enthusiasm for the adventure cooling as rapidly as her body. 'They haven't given up, though?'

'Of course not, although they're pretty stretched at the moment, what with organising security for a couple of royal visits and the hunt for Carole Prescot's killer.'

'The "Sex Strangler"?'

'Ah . . . well . . .'

It was immediately clear he was holding something back. Melissa pounced. 'Do they think it was someone else?'

'This hasn't been made public yet,' said Bruce, after a moment's hesitation, 'so for Pete's sake don't let on I've told you. I learned off the record that they're pretty sure Carole *wasn't* killed by the Strangler, but by someone who tried to make it look like his MO. According to the PM, the pressure on her throat wasn't applied in the same way – remember, the Strangler knows how to render his victims temporarily unconscious without killing them. There were differences in the way her hands and feet had been tied as well, although only minor ones. A granny knot instead of a reef . . . that sort of thing.'

'That would suggest it wasn't a random attack. Someone had a specific motive for killing her.'

'That's the line they're working on at present, but it's the motive that's baffling them. She seems to have led a blameless sort of existence, not mixed with any dodgy company or taken drugs. For the time being, the fuzz are keeping their thoughts to themselves to avoid putting the murderer on his guard.'

'Poor girl,' said Melissa softly. 'She had such a shy, gentle manner. Why would anyone want to kill her?'

Bruce turned his head in surprise. 'You knew her?'

'I met her once . . . no, a couple of times . . . in Mr Semple's office.'

'Charlie Semple – the solicitor?'

'We didn't get on first name terms, but I imagine it's the same man. The firm is Rathbone and Semple.'

'That's him. Is he your solicitor?'

'No, he's handling Leonora Jewell's estate. I went to his office to meet her executor before we all went off to her cottage to collect the manuscript. It turned into rather a creepy experience – I haven't told you about that, have I?' She described the visit and its aftermath; he listened attentively, chuckling over the clashes between Semple and Round, but growing serious when she described finding what she believed to be the murder weapon in the well, its disappearance and her subsequent brush with Inspector Holloway. 'So how come you know Semple?' she asked when she had finished her story.

'I don't really know him, but I've seen him down at the nick a few times. He and his partners are on a rota for when someone in custody asks for a brief.'

'I see.' Melissa thought for a moment, then said wistfully,

149

'Carole phoned me the day before she was killed and asked to meet me. If only I knew what she wanted to talk about, it might give the police a clue. I reported the call, of course, but unless she confided in someone else they won't get far.'

They fell silent again, concentrating on their vigil. After a further five minutes had crept past, during which Melissa felt as if the circulation in her feet had stopped for ever, she became aware of Bruce tensing beside her, like a predator that has spotted its prey.

'They're on the move, the lights have gone out,' he said, rolling down the window. A blast of cold air hit them; Melissa gasped and pulled her woollen cap over her ears, but Bruce seemed impervious to the drop in temperature. 'Listen!' he commanded.

Borne towards them on the wind came the sound of a motor starting up. Headlights shone briefly in their direction, then swung in an arc as the car made its way along the drive that encircled the Hall and headed towards the main gates. As it did so, powerful lights came on at intervals around the building.

'They were triggered as the car went past,' Bruce explained. 'They'll go out in a minute or two.' It seemed like ten to Melissa, but eventually the place was once more in darkness. 'Right, we're on our way. Don't slam the doors when you get out. Keep close to me and mind how you go. The ground may be bumpy in places.'

They had parked opposite a gate into a field that lay between the grounds of the Hall and the lane. They clambered over it and Bruce set off across the uneven grass with Melissa at his heels. 'How do you know which direction to take?' she panted. 'It's almost pitch dark. Suppose we wander off course and trigger the lights?'

'We're not in range of the sensors yet. There's a wall separating this field from the rear gardens of the house. Growing against the other side is an ash tree; we make for that.'

'I don't see any tree.'

'That's because it's in a direct line with the house, so it doesn't stand out.'

'So how do we find it?'

'We work our way along the wall. Here we are.'

Stumbling over a tuft of grass, Melissa almost fell against the rough, uneven stones. The hands that she put out to save herself were numb, despite her thick gloves.

'Which way?' she asked.

'To the right. You can see the tree now.'

So she could. A black silhouette seemed to have risen out of the ground, its branches flailing and creaking in the wind. They made their way towards it.

'Okay,' said Bruce. 'I'll go first and give you a hand. The wall's quite low and it's got a smooth top, so it shouldn't be difficult.'

In broad daylight, it would have been relatively easy. In these conditions, Melissa felt as if she was being asked to climb a cliff. 'Why didn't you bring a torch?' she grumbled.

'I did, but I'd rather not use it here. Someone might be looking out of one of the farmhouse windows and spot it.'

Convinced that she was ruining a perfectly good anorak and ski pants, Melissa managed to find a foothold and heave herself on to the flat coping stone. Bruce caught her by the shoulders and half guided, half lifted her down on the other side. 'Okay?' he whispered.

'I suppose so. Now what?'

They were close enough to the building to pick out individual features. 'See that row of white stone, level with the first floor windows?' said Bruce. 'That's the parapet running round the roof that Gerard's flat looks out on. We make straight for that corner. There's a lawn and then a gravel path. Keep close behind me and crouch down as low as you can.'

Melissa expected to be blinded by floodlights at any moment, but it seemed that Bruce had got his calculations exactly right. Soon they were standing in the deep shadow made by the angle between the main building and the single-storey extension.

'So far, so good,' said Bruce. 'Now, where did I see those ladders? There were two of them.' He moved away; a few seconds later he called, 'Here they are! Come and give me a hand. Keep close to the wall – the sensors are angled outwards.'

As Melissa moved in the direction of his voice, the world became dramatically brighter and she only just managed to check a cry of alarm. Then she gave a slightly hysterical laugh as she realised that what she had mistaken for floodlighting was in fact the moon, unexpectedly breaking through a gap torn in the clouds by the rising wind.

'Great,' said Bruce. 'Now we can see what we're doing. Grab hold of that and fold it up or something.'

'That' was what seemed like half a mile of black plastic sheeting in which the ladders had been swathed. As Melissa struggled to reduce it to a manageable package, a playful gust of wind first wrapped one end round her head and shoulders and then seized the other and flung it in the air, where it hovered, flapping and rustling, like the wings of a monstrous bat. Somehow, she got it under control and anchored it under one of the ladders while Bruce extended the second. Between them, they managed to get it into position.

'It's a bit shorter than I expected,' Bruce remarked as he tested it for stability, 'but I think it'll do. I'll lead the way.'

Clouds were again obscuring the moon so that in no time he was nothing but a vague shape above her head. Then his voice floated down through the darkness, 'Okay, it's a piece of cake. Come on up.'

As she gripped the sides of the ladder and began her ascent, an agonising question swept into Melissa's mind: *Going up's*

going to be bad enough, but how the hell do I get down again?
Driven by Bruce's persuasive enthusiasm and her own wish to
bring Leonora Jewell's killer to book, she had overlooked one
of her own weaknesses: vertigo. The prospect of lowering herself
backwards over that low parapet, feet groping in a void for a
ladder that she could not see because she dare not, even for a
moment, look down, sent her head into a sickening spin. It was
too late now, she was committed, but the prospect made her
knees tremble so much that she could barely move. Her hands
and forehead became clammy with sweat despite the cold.

'Get a move on!' came an impatient voice above her.

To go on meant facing a terrifying ordeal; to back out now
would mean being branded a coward. She chose the lesser evil.
'Coming!' she called back through chattering teeth.

Somehow, she reached the top of the ladder. Another brief
spell of moonlight illuminated the parapet and with a gasp of
relief she grabbed at one of the slender pillars that supported
the coping. 'Give me your hand and climb over,' ordered Bruce.
Dumbly, she obeyed; the next minute she stood erect beside
him.

The roof was about thirty feet square, bounded on two sides
by the walls of the house. There were two pairs of windows, one
pair facing west and the other north. All were in darkness.
Cautiously, Bruce switched on his torch; the west-facing
windows were curtained, but the narrow beam shone straight
through the others into what was obviously a workroom. They
saw a long bench with a few hand-tools neatly arranged in a
rack and below it what appeared to be an assortment of empty
picture frames. There were two rolls of off-white material at
one end, and on a table at right angles to the bench lay two or
three blank prepared canvases. Beside them was something
covered with a piece of cloth.

'Wonder what that is?' said Melissa.

'Let's see if we can find out.' Bruce was examining the old-fashioned sash windows. 'I think we're in luck. Hold this.' He passed her the torch, took a Swiss army knife from his pocket and clicked out a flat, narrow blade. He inserted it between the top and bottom sections of one of the windows and attempted to lever the catch sideways, but it would not budge.

'No good,' he muttered. 'I'll try the other one.'

After a brief tussle, the second one yielded. Between them, the two amateur burglars managed to raise the lower frame far enough for them to clamber over the sill into the room. They made for the table; Bruce lifted the cloth and directed the torch at what lay underneath.

'What do you make of that?' he asked.

Melissa stared down at the picture. It was a simple seascape: a sandy beach beneath a summer sky flecked with clouds, low cliffs, scattered rocks, a solitary figure trudging along a shore and two children playing at the edge of a glass-green sea. Simple, but painted by a master. She looked for, and found, a signature.

'I thought so!' she exclaimed. 'It's a Boudin!'

'Is it valuable?'

'It's worth a fortune, if it's genuine. He was a leading Impressionist. This is the beach at Trouville, one of his favourite subjects.'

'So it's unlikely to have been donated to finance an AFTER project?'

'Highly unlikely. I'd say it was even money this is one of the works pinched from Rillingford Manor.'

'What about those?' Bruce indicated the blank canvases.

Melissa picked one up and studied it, then turned it over. 'I think this is what you'd call a mulberry sandwich,' she said. 'Look, the back of the canvas is darker than the front, and a different texture. Iris was right!' The two exchanged excited glances.

154

'It seems we've got what we came for,' said Bruce. 'D'you mind holding this?' He passed her the torch, fumbled in his pocket and took out a small automatic camera. 'We'd better not risk switching on the light, so try and keep the torch steady.' There was a succession of flashes as he took half-a-dozen shots, then put the camera away and covered up the canvas.

'Right, let's make tracks before Gerard and Eloise get back.'

They climbed out through the window and closed it behind them. With the knife, Bruce slid the catch back into place and then led the way to where the ladder stood waiting for them. 'Want me to go first, or will you?'

In the thrill of discovery, Melissa had temporarily forgotten what lay ahead. Now, the horror was staring her in the face. She closed her eyes and turned away.

'I can't go down there,' she whispered.

'What?'

'I shouldn't have come. I get vertigo – I can't stand heights.'

'Heights? It's only twenty feet or so.'

'I can't do it.'

'Don't be so wet!'

The words stung. 'You don't know what it's like,' she whimpered.

'Look, either you climb down that ladder or you'll be left up here on your own,' he snapped back.

'You can't do that,' she pleaded in a panic.

'Watch me.' He made for the parapet, looked down to check the position of the ladder, grasped the coping with both hands and swung first one leg and then the other across it. 'Look, it's as easy as getting into the bath,' he said. 'Do exactly as I'm doing and you'll be fine.'

In all the time she had known him, despite the teasing and coaxing and the adventures they had shared, he had always treated her with a certain deference. Now, he was unmistakably in charge. There was a note of authority in his voice that helped to steady her. 'I'll try,' she faltered.

'Good girl. I'll go halfway down and wait for you.'

His head and shoulders disappeared and the panic returned in a knotted lump, like a balled fist that threatened to rise into her throat and choke her. 'Wait for me! Stay where I can see you!' she croaked.

'I'm right here. Do exactly as I did; I'll grab your feet and guide them on to the ladder,' he called back.

She felt as if every part of her nervous system was coming unravelled. Gritting her teeth and closing her eyes, clinging to the coping as if it was all that stood between her and eternity, she managed to get her left leg over it and began groping with her foot on the other side. It met emptiness.

'I can't find the ladder,' she moaned.

'You're too far out. Edge towards the wall a bit.'

With an effort she wriggled forward an inch or so, terrified that at any moment she would lose her grip and fall. Then a hand grasped her ankle and she felt something solid under her foot.

'Okay, got you! Now the other one.'

Never, she vowed to herself as she struggled to control a limb that had turned into lead, *never again will I get myself into anything like this*.

'That's fine,' Bruce was saying. 'You're on the ladder. Hang on to the parapet and come down a rung or two. That's it. One more. Now let go of the parapet with one hand at a time and hold the sides of the ladder. Come on, you're okay, I won't let you fall.'

It was like descending into a bottomless pit; several aeons passed before the earth was firm beneath her feet. Still clinging to the ladder, she hid her face in her arms, almost sobbing with relief.

Bruce gave her a brotherly pat on the shoulder. 'Well done,' he said.

'I feel such a fool . . .' she gulped.

'Forget it. We all have our weaknesses . . . I can't stand spiders. Come on, let's put this away.'

They lowered the ladder and laid it on the ground with the other one. While Bruce replaced the plastic cover, Melissa held the torch, gripping it with hands that would not stop trembling.

When he had finished, Bruce checked the luminous face of his wristwatch. 'Not quite eight o'clock,' he said. 'That was pretty good going. Let's get back to the car.'

Before they could move a step, they were enveloped in a sheet of dazzling light. But this time, it was not the moon. An approaching vehicle had activated the security system.

Chapter Nineteen

There was no cover and no chance of reaching the boundary wall without being spotted.

'Crouch in the corner and keep your face covered,' hissed Bruce in Melissa's ear. 'It's a circular drive – if they approach from the other direction there's a good chance they won't see us.'

'Who d'you suppose it is?' she whispered as they cowered in the shadows while the car drew rapidly closer.

'No idea. Burglars, perhaps. Think we should call the police?'

Melissa, still shaky from her ordeal on the ladder, could barely hear his voice above the pounding of her own heart. 'Not funny. This lot's putting years on me,' she muttered.

'Listen! They've stopped. I think we're in luck.'

She raised her head a fraction and squinted through her fingers. The car had pulled up a short distance away, out of sight, but very close to their hiding place. She heard the engine ticking over; one of the doors was flung open and then violently slammed, as if by someone in a furious temper. A few quick footsteps sounded on the gravel and stopped. There were faint jingling and scraping sounds.

'Get a move on!' roared a man's voice. He must have lowered the window, for the sound was clear and unmuffled.

'That's Gerard,' whispered Bruce. 'What's going on?'

They heard a metallic tinkle and a light thud, as if something had fallen to the ground, followed by a woman's voice exclaiming, 'Shit, I've dropped the sodding keys!'

'And that's Eloise. What happened to the posh accent?'

'You clumsy cow!' shouted Gerard.

'They're having a fair old run-in by the sound of it,' chuckled Bruce. 'Something must have gone wrong.'

There were more sounds of fumbling with keys, then the rasp of metal on metal followed by a click as an up-and-over door swung open, accompanied by a snarl of, 'About bloody time!' The engine revved, faded and died as the car was driven into the garage. 'Well don't stand there gawping,' bellowed Gerard. 'Shut the door. Can't you do anything useful?'

'Shut it your bloody self!' Eloise's voice was shrill with rage; all pretence at gentility had vanished. 'I'm not your slave.'

'If you were I'd sell you pretty damn quick. You're about as much use as a torn French letter. You can't even make a restaurant booking without ballsing it up.'

'It wasn't my fault, I tell you. The girl who took the booking was foreign, she must have got the date wrong.'

'Oh sure, it's always the other person's fault. One more cock-up like that, and you're fired.'

'You can't get rid of me, I know too much.'

'What?' Gerard's voice took on a new, menacing note. 'Don't you threaten me, or I'll . . .'

The listeners were never to know what penalty Eloise risked paying, for at that point the garage door was slammed down. At the same moment, the security lights went out.

'Let's make a dash for it while they're on their way upstairs,' said Bruce. 'Can you see the ash tree?'

'Just about.'

'Head for that. Try and keep in a straight line to avoid the sensors. Ready?'

'As I'll ever be.'

'Go!'

He was considerably younger than she was, and no doubt a good deal fitter. She stumbled after him, desperately trying to keep up, conscious that her legs were stiff from the minutes spent crouching in the corner and that she was rapidly running out of breath. Halfway across the grass she missed her footing, almost fell and ran wide. In an instant the floodlights came on.

For the second time that evening, panic set in. She could just see Bruce some yards ahead of her, running like a deer, fading into the penumbra and then vanishing altogether. Desperately, she toiled after him, terrified that at any second there would be a hue and cry. The ground sloped gently upwards between the house and the boundary wall; she had barely noticed the gradient on the way in, but in her semi-exhausted state it felt almost vertical.

Somehow, she reached the wall and collapsed against it. There was a stitch in her side, her head was swimming and her breath laboured; she was almost spent.

'Quick, get over!' said Bruce's voice. 'I'll give you a hand.'

Using what she was convinced must be her last ounce of strength, she managed to heave herself on top of the flat coping stone and drop down on the other side. Because of the lie of the land, it was further than she expected and she would have fallen if Bruce had not grabbed her.

'That was close,' he said.

'Are they after us?' she panted.

'I don't think so. The lights have gone out again.' From a semi-crouching position, he peered over the wall like a sniper over a parapet. 'No, I think our luck's held. Ten to one they were still so busy shouting at each other they never noticed a thing. Let's get back to the car.'

'Give me a minute or two to get my breath. I'm not so fit as you.'

'All right, there's no rush now.'

'Just as well. I couldn't run any further to save my life. I nearly blew it again, didn't I? I'm sorry . . .'

'Not necessarily. It could easily have been me who triggered the lights,' said Bruce gallantly. He sounded as relaxed and unruffled as if they were having a drink in a pub.

'Nice of you to say so.'

'Forget it. The main thing is, we did it?' He punched the air like a footballer who has just scored a goal. 'Unless Gerard uses a slide rule to check where he leaves everything in his workshop, he'll never know anyone's been in there. Are those two in for a shock when the fuzz turn up with their search warrant!'

'I sure hope so. I'd hate to think we've done all this for nothing.' She got to her feet and brushed herself down. 'I'm okay now. Shall we go?'

As she settled thankfully into her seat and buckled her safety belt, a disturbing thought struck her. 'Bruce, d'you think Gerard's likely to hurt Eloise? You heard what she said – she could be a real danger to him.'

'He might slap her about a bit, just to teach her a lesson. He won't kill her, if that's what you're worried about – she's too useful.'

'You're right. She's probably the only one who can handle Arnie. They can't afford to have him upset.'

'Arnie must have seemed like a gift from the gods,' agreed Bruce. 'They couldn't let a normal artist get his hands on those doctored canvases.' He started the engine, switched on the headlights and pulled on to the road.

'What a bit of luck it was that Iris spotted that one.' Gleefully, Melissa rubbed her hands together. 'If it wasn't for her, we'd never have got this far. She'll be tickled pink when she hears what we've found out.'

They reached the junction with the main road. 'I don't know about you, but I'm starving,' said Bruce. 'There must be somewhere to eat near here.'

'Are you kidding? We can't go into a restaurant looking like a couple of scarecrows.'

'No, I suppose not. Any ideas?'

'Do you want to come back to my place and clean up? I'll dig something out of the freezer.'

'Great.'

Less than an hour later they were eating spaghetti Bolognese and drinking red Chianti in Melissa's kitchen.

'Here's to the downfall of the inventors of the mulberry sandwich!' said Bruce, raising his glass. ' "Mulberry Sandwich",' he repeated musingly. 'That'd make an intriguing title for one of your mysteries, wouldn't it?'

'It might.' Melissa drank, then thought of another toast. 'And here's to . . . oh, damn!'

'What's wrong?'

'Leonora.'

'What about her?'

'Don't you see? All we've done this evening is find confirmation of what we already suspected – Gerard and Eloise are handling stolen paintings. We're no nearer proving that they had anything to do with Leonora's death.'

'That's true. Still, there's enough circumstantial evidence to give the police a lead in that direction.'

'And what about Carole Prescot's murder?'

'Carole?' Bruce looked puzzled. 'What makes you think there's a connection?'

'I don't know.' Melissa frowned, trying to retrace her own train of thought. 'I suppose it's because she happened to work for Leonora's solicitor . . . and because there was something she badly wanted to talk to me about.'

'If it had been anything to do with Leonora, the obvious person to talk to would have been her own boss.'

'Of course. There's no logical reason to suppose there's a link. Anyway, how are you going to handle this?'

'I'll get the pics processed tomorrow and pass them to the Super. He's masterminding the art theft enquiries. I'll tell him what Arnie said about giving a picture to the "writing lady" and see what his reaction is.'

'I doubt if Arnie would be of much value as a witness.'

'No, but you and Iris both heard what he said, and you can confirm that Leonora went to Blackwater Hall . . .'

'Me?' Melissa looked up in alarm. 'I'd rather stay out of this, if you don't mind.'

'You can't stay out of it. You're a key witness to what we saw in Gerard's workshop.'

'But you've got the photographs . . .'

'There'd only be my word for it that I took them in Blackwater Hall. What's the problem?'

'I don't want Ken Harris to know what I've been up to. He'd go ballistic.'

'Burst all his stitches!' Bruce chuckled. 'Okay, I'll try refusing to reveal my sources, but I can't guarantee I'll get away with it.'

'I'd be very grateful if you would.'

They finished their pasta. Melissa fetched fruit and cheese, filled the kettle and put it on the stove. While she was preparing coffee, Bruce pulled out a notebook and pencil. He jotted down a few words and then sat staring straight ahead, his chin leaning on one hand while he made elaborate doodles with the other.

'Penny for 'em,' she said as she put a cup of coffee in front of him.

'Huh? Sorry, I was miles away.' He closed the notebook and slipped it into his pocket.

'You've had an idea, haven't you?' He spooned sugar into his coffee and stirred it without replying. 'Oh, come on!' she begged. 'Don't hold out on me.'

He shook his head. 'It may be nothing . . . it's only a vague idea . . .'

'What?'

'I'd rather not say anything until I've done some checks. It could be just a red herring.'

'They're my speciality. Bruce, you can't do this!'

He drank his coffee, put down the cup and stood up, glancing at his watch. 'Is that the time? I'm keeping you up . . . thanks for the meal, it was great.'

'You're a heel. You drag me out on a crazy adventure, I nearly break my neck . . . and then you clam up on me.'

He grinned, but would not be drawn. 'I'll be in touch. You go to bed now like a good girl. You've had enough excitement for one day.'

Shortly after Bruce left, Ken Harris rang. 'Where have you been?' he demanded querulously. 'I called twice during the evening and there was no reply, no answering machine . . .'

'I'm sorry, I forgot to switch it on before I went out. How are you feeling?'

'Bored. I was hoping you'd find time to come and see me.'

'Ken, it's nearly a hundred miles from here to Southampton. The return drive alone could take five hours, and I'm up to my eyes in work.'

'You weren't too busy to go out for the evening.'

And why the hell shouldn't I take a couple of hours off? I'm not accountable to you. Remembering that he was still weak after surgery, she checked the indignant retort.

'I wasn't out for long, and it was partly work,' she said soothingly. 'I was interviewing someone for my book,' she improvised, praying that he would not ask for chapter and verse. At that moment she was incapable of concocting a convincing story off the top of her head; the evening's excitement had left her brain in a state of seething confusion. Mercifully, he let it drop.

'As long as you're all right. I worry about you. That cottage is so isolated . . .'

'I'm fine,' she assured him. 'Have you seen the doctor today? Are you definitely being moved to Cheltenham on Friday?'

'Yes and yes. You'll come and see me there, won't you?' He sounded like a small boy wanting reassurance.

'Of course I will.'

'Mel, when I'm out of hospital, I want to talk about us.'

'What is there to talk about?' *You shouldn't have said that. Now he'll lie awake half the night fretting.* 'I mean, we're fine as we are, surely,' she added hurriedly, trying to undo the damage.

'You know very well what I mean.' His voice had a hint of a tremor; he was becoming emotional. 'Mel, I care about you so much.'

'I know.' She felt her own throat tightening. 'Look, Ken, don't worry. When you come home, we'll have a long talk, I promise. I care too,' she added before she could stop herself.

'That's all I wanted to hear.' Immediately, his voice became firmer. 'I'll talk to you tomorrow. Good-night, darling.'

'Good-night.'

It was the first time he had called her that. It marked a new stage in their relationship, one she was not certain she was ready for.

Her normal bedtime drink was a cup of tea, but tonight, feeling in need of something stronger, she polished off what was left of the Chianti. One way and another, it had been quite an evening.

Chapter Twenty

Melissa awoke early the next morning after a deep but troubled sleep, during which her dreams had been haunted by the eyes of Leonora Jewell. They were in the otherwise featureless faces of passers-by as she hurried through crowded streets and in and out of shops, looking for something she could not find because she did not know what it was; she glimpsed them among the passengers on a train which was taking her to an unknown destination; they stared up at her from the pages of books whose covers bore no titles.

Dawn had not yet broken. Through her bedroom window she looked out on a landscape coated with silver by the moonlight. The wind had died, leaving the trees motionless against a sky ablaze with stars that sparkled like chips of ice. She put on her dressing-gown and slippers, went to the kitchen and made a pot of tea. Binkie, curled up in his usual corner, raised his head and blinked at her, yawning, before getting up and making purposefully for the back door. She unlocked it and held it open for him, shivering in the tide of frosty air that rolled into the room.

'Get a move on!' she commanded as the cat hesitated before stepping reluctantly outside. She closed the door behind him, filled a mug with tea and took it upstairs. After drinking it she showered, put on a warm jersey and leggings and went to her study to begin her working day.

The first thing she noticed as she sat down at her desk was the copy of Leonora's novel that she had been reading earlier. It lay on the desk beside the word processor, face down. 'I could have sworn I put you back on the shelf,' she muttered as she caught the eye of the author looking up at her from the dust jacket. Previously its expression had seemed reproachful; this morning, there appeared to be a trace of disappointment in its mute gaze.

'For heaven's sake, leave me alone!' Melissa exclaimed. 'I nearly broke my neck yesterday evening, trying to turn up a clue to your killer. What else do you expect me to do?'

Without realising it, she had snatched up the book and addressed the portrait aloud. The paper eyes had an intense, compelling expression that conveyed something of the strength and vigour of the living woman. For a moment, Melissa had the uncanny, irrational, but powerful impression that the picture wanted to speak; she found herself saying, 'What are you trying to tell me?' Then, reproaching herself for a fanciful idiot, she thrust the book back on the shelf with the others and determinedly switched her thoughts to the next chapter of *Deadly Legacy*.

It came easily. The words streamed out of her head, through her fingertips and on to the screen as if driven by a force outside her control. At this rate, she would soon be approaching the *dénouement*, where the amateur art-lover hero – who had spent several hundred pages and tackled countless hair-raising situations in his pursuit of a missing painting, bequeathed to the heroine and seemingly the target of every crook in Europe – would at last be in a position to expose the arch-villain and retrieve the priceless masterpiece that had travelled halfway round the world concealed in the false bottom of a cabin trunk.

'I must say,' said Melissa to herself as she re-read the plot

170

outline to make sure she had included all the essential details, 'that seems a pretty mundane sort of hiding place. Couldn't you have thought of something more original than that, Leonora?'

She did think of something more original, said a voice in her head. *She invented the mulberry sandwich. Only that crook Gerard Hood said it wasn't feasible.*

'But it *is* feasible, Iris said so! And Bruce and I have all but proved it.'

The words, spoken forcefully and aloud, rang round the room. Melissa sat back in her chair and clapped her hands to her face in sheer exasperation. There *must* be a connection between the Blackwater scam and Leonora's murder. If only the dead author had made a written record of her idea and of her visits to Sam Deacon and Gerard Hood. She was such a stickler for detail in other matters; why omit something so significant?

'Perhaps she did make notes, and then destroyed them after Gerard scotched the idea,' Melissa muttered disconsolately.

She checked the clock on her desk. It was half-past nine; she had been writing for almost three hours and daylight had arrived unnoticed. She switched off the electric lamp and opened the curtains, aware that her back and shoulders were stiff and her stomach empty. She went downstairs to prepare some breakfast.

While she was eating, the telephone rang.

'Mrs Craig?' said a man's voice. It sounded familiar, but she could not put a name to it.

'Who's that?' she asked.

'Jonathan Round here. I hope I'm not interrupting your work . . . I wasn't sure when would be the best time to call you.'

'It's all right, you've caught me taking a break. What can I do for you?'

'Er, nothing really, that is, I just wondered how you were getting on with Leonora's book.'

171

'Quite well, as a matter of fact. I've drafted one chapter and sent it to her editor for comments, and I'm working on the next.'

'Splendid.'

There was a pause, neither immediately able to think of anything to say, before Melissa had a moment of inspiration. With hindsight, she wondered why on earth it had not occurred to her before.

'Mr Round, did your godmother by any chance keep a diary? A personal diary, I mean, not research notes for individual books.'

'She did indeed. She didn't call it a diary, though, she called it something else . . . a commentary . . . no, that doesn't sound right . . .'

'A commonplace book?'

'That's it! It wasn't just a record of her daily doings – it was that as well, of course – but she used to include all sorts of odds and ends in it: recipes, notes of work she'd done in the garden, ideas for plots and so on.'

'Have you got it?'

'No, I haven't. I never gave it a thought. The shock and upset of her death . . . I still haven't decided what to do about her things or whether to sell the cottage . . .' His voice trailed jerkily away.

It was plain that he had been very attached to his eccentric godmother. Melissa felt a rush of sympathy for him and gave him a moment to compose himself before asking, 'Do you happen know where she kept it?'

'In a little compartment at the back of the top drawer of her desk. I imagine it's still there – unless the police found it and took it away. I can't imagine what interest it would have had for them, though. Why do you ask?'

Melissa decided that a bowdlerised version of the truth would be sufficient. 'I came across a passing reference in her research notes to a possible change she was considering to the ending of *Deadly Legacy*,' she said carefully. 'I thought it might be worth investigating, and I know for a fact that she asked one or two people whether her idea would work, but I can't find any other mention of it and it occurred to me . . .'

Jonathan Round took up the suggestion immediately.

' . . . that she might have recorded it in her diary!' He sounded quite excited. 'I think it's more than likely. Why don't you have a word with old Semple? He'd know if it was with the things the police took from Quarry Cottage. If it wasn't, it must still be there.'

'Would it be all right if I went to look for it?'

'Of course. Semple still has the keys. Tell him you've spoken to me and I've agreed.'

'Thank you very much.'

'Not at all. Let me know if you turn up anything useful, won't you?'

Melissa's heart was racing with excitement as she put the phone down. If she could lay her hands on that book . . . if it was up to date . . . if Leonora had written up her visit to Blackwater Hall and her interview with Gerard Hood . . . possibly recorded her encounter with Arnie and the gift of the picture . . . maybe even made a note of attempts to reclaim it . . . a dizzying sequence, leading to irrefutable evidence connecting Hood with Leonora's death, formed in her head like a trail laid for runners in a cross-country race. She flew back upstairs, checked the telephone number of Rathbone and Semple, called it and asked to speak to the senior partner.

She was put straight through to Miss Gudgeon. It crossed her mind, as she made her request, that this rather daunting woman, with her self-confident manner and fashionable, well-cut clothes, was the type one might expect to come across in advertising or public relations rather than in the office of a rather old-fashioned solicitor. There was no warmth in her manner as she explained that Mr Semple was in court and would not be in the office until midday. On learning the reason for Melissa's call, she adopted a dismissive, almost hostile tone.

'I couldn't possibly take the responsibility for handing over the keys without proper authority,' she said flatly.

'But I have permission from Miss Jewell's executor,' Melissa pointed out. 'Surely that's sufficient authority for you?'

'Without wishing to give offence, I only have your word for that.'

'Then why don't you give Mr Round a call and check with him?'

'I think it would be better if you waited and spoke to Mr Semple.'

'But you just told me he may not be in until after lunch. That diary may contain important information to help me with Miss Jewell's book. I am working to a deadline, you know, and if it means making changes I need to know right away.'

'I'm sorry, but you'll have to wait until you can clear it with Mr Semple. Give me your number and I'll get back to you as soon as he comes in.'

There was no point in arguing. Melissa gave her number and put down the phone, grinding her teeth in frustration. Thoroughly disgruntled and in no mood to continue working, she put on her outdoor clothes and went for a walk, wishing that Iris was there to keep her company and to sympathise while she held forth on the subject of over-zealous secretaries.

When she returned an hour later there was a message on her answering machine, asking her to call Mr Semple. A moment later she was speaking to him.

'I understood you wouldn't be in until this afternoon,' she began.

'My client's case had to be adjourned; a key witness has been taken ill,' he explained. 'What can I do for you, Mrs Craig?'

'Didn't your secretary explain?'

'She told me you wish to go to Quarry Cottage, but she didn't say why.'

For the second time, Melissa explained about the diary. He listened without interruption; when she had finished he said, 'How interesting. I had no idea that Miss Jewell kept such a record. Of course, she was a very private person. I wonder how much it will reveal about her? I daresay it would be of considerable interest to a future biographer.'

'It might even be of interest to the police,' said Melissa impulsively. It occurred to her at that moment that Mr Semple could be a useful ally if the diary revealed anything she felt worth reporting. If she could get him on her side, DI Holloway might treat her with a little more respect.

'The police?' The solicitor sounded puzzled. 'What are you expecting to find?'

'I have a hunch – I'd rather not go into details now, it's all too vague and too involved – but I don't believe Leonora was killed by a casual intruder. I think she was killed because she had accidentally come by something extremely valuable.'

'You're suggesting she was deliberately murdered?' Mr Semple was clearly appalled at the idea. 'Have you any evidence . . . do you know what that something was?'

'A picture.'

'What picture?'

'I don't know that. I don't know anything for certain, but I think her diary may contain something to confirm what I'm saying.'

'So what you told Miss Gudgeon about a change to her plot wasn't the real reason . . .'

'Oh yes, it was, truly.' Melissa had the feeling that she had lost Brownie points for not telling the whole truth at the outset. 'I've been trying to find out just what Leonora was planning . . . it wasn't in her original plot outline . . . and I've come across something . . . it's very complicated, but I believe her research led her into something illegal that's going on at Blackwater Hall, quite innocently, of course, I don't think for a moment that she realised . . . if I could just get a look at her diary, there may be something in it that ties the whole thing together.' The words tumbled out in a rush and she experienced an enormous sense of relief at unburdening herself to someone of Mr Semple's standing. She was on the point of going on to confess her escapade with Bruce the previous evening, but decided not to. He could hardly approve, and it would only cloud the issue.

'This sounds quite unbelievable,' the solicitor was saying. 'I cannot conceive of Miss Jewell having anything to do with illegal activities. And where is this Blackwater Hall?'

'It's an art centre near Gloucester. I'm sure Leonora . . . Miss Jewell . . . had absolutely no idea . . . look, may I please have the keys and go and look for the diary? It may give us some of the answers.'

'Yes, yes, of course.' He sounded abstracted, as if he was trying to gather his thoughts and make sense of what she had been saying. 'When do you want to pick them up?'

'I can come right away, if that's all right with you. Say, in half an hour?'

'Very well. Have you any idea where to look?'

'Mr Round said she kept it in her desk, at the back of one of the drawers.'

'Does Mr Round know of your suspicions, by the way?'

'No. Do you think I should have told him?'

'Unless it becomes absolutely necessary, I think it's better he knows nothing of this. He was very fond of his godmother and we don't want to distress him.'

'I quite agree. I'll see you shortly, then.'

Melissa's skin was tingling with anticipation as she drove along the track leading to Quarry Cottage. When she pulled up outside, she sat for a moment in contemplation. Her first sight of the place had been in mild autumn sunshine; today the sky was covered with leaden clouds that hinted at snow and gave it a desolate, almost sinister appearance. Already the garden was starting to look neglected. The trim lawns had ragged edges. Someone delivering junk mail had failed to push it through the letter-box, leaving loose sheets of gaudily-coloured paper to blow into the bushes, where they hung like tattered washing on a line. The coconut shell dangled empty from the apple tree, and the birdbath contained nothing but a few sodden leaves. More leaves were scattered on the flower beds, where thousands of weeds had germinated in defiance of the cold.

'Poor Leonora,' said Melissa sadly. 'It'd break your heart to see it looking like this.'

Recalling that backing the Golf on to the narrow track on leaving had not been easy, she took the precaution of reversing through the rickety gate to enable her to drive straight out. She sat in the car for several moments after switching off the engine. Despite her eagerness to get her hands on Leonora's diary, she felt an unexpected reluctance to enter the cottage. She had never experienced any supernatural manifestations, and certainly there had been nothing spooky about the atmosphere on her previous visit, but on that occasion she had been in the company of three stalwart men. It crossed her mind that it would have been a good idea to invite Bruce to accompany her. Then she told herself not to be a fool.

'Come on, girl, get on with it. You don't imagine Leonora's haunting the place, do you?'

Just the same, her heart was thumping as she got out of the car, walked up to the front door of the cottage, opened it with the key that an unsmiling Miss Gudgeon had, with apparent reluctance, handed over, and stepped inside.

Chapter Twenty-One

It was cold in Quarry Cottage, much colder than Melissa remembered. It was only natural, of course; the place had been standing empty for a further two weeks, during which the weather had, in the way of things in England in autumn, see-sawed between rain, a few hours of sunshine tempered with chilly winds, and sharp overnight frosts. Any warmth from the sunny spells had failed to penetrate the thick stone walls, and the air inside had a dankness which made her shiver as she made her way along the passage to the room which had served Leonora as both sitting-room and study.

Everything looked the same: the small windows divided by wooden bars into even smaller panes, the faded curtains, the shabby furniture, the alcove overlooking the garden where Leonora had worked, the stone hearth where she had died, the brown stain where her blood had trickled on to the carpet . . . Melissa swallowed hard to stave off a spasm of nausea and her knees began to tremble. She felt an urgent desire to do what she had come for and get away as soon as possible.

The desk was a plain wooden affair with three drawers to one side. Melissa pulled the top one open; it appeared to contain nothing but a quantity of plain typing paper, but by groping at the back she found the narrow compartment of which Jonathan Round had spoken, separated from the rest by a thin partition. Her heart began to thump again, this time with excitement and anticipation, as her exploring hand brought out a thick notebook with a hard blue cover. She opened it and began turning over pages covered in a flowing handwriting that was surprisingly firm for a woman turned eighty.

On September the second, Leonora had written:

Jonathan telephoned to say he's off to Greece tomorrow and will I be all right while he's away. I know he means it kindly but I do wish he wouldn't fuss. I may be old but I'm not decrepit yet. Mrs Finch is the same. She keeps saying I should think about going into what she calls 'sheltered housing'. The very idea! How could I work with other people around me all the time? And how could I live without my garden?

'How typical – but what a pity you didn't take Mrs Finch's advice,' Melissa murmured sadly. 'You might still be alive today. But you're right, you'd have hated it,' she added, glancing out of the window in time to see two male blackbirds engaged in a fierce mid-air squabble. 'This was your entire world.'

The next few pages of the diary were filled with brief notes of jobs done in the garden, plans for future planting, a record of work carried out by Mrs Finch – evidently Leonora's domestic help – observations on wild life, hints on slug control offered by Mr Finch. There were a few passing references to *Deadly Legacy* on the lines of, '*Chapter two is giving me some problems*' or – here Melissa found herself smiling in sympathy – '*my wretched heroine will not do as I tell her!*' There was, however, nothing of any real significance or relevance to the mystery until an entry dated a few days before Leonora's death. '*Today I had an absolute brainwave!*' she had written. '*If only it's feasible, it will be a*

<u>much</u> more interesting and original way of hiding the picture than that old cabin trunk. I must make some enquiries <u>right away</u>.'

As she read the words, some heavily underscored, Melissa could sense and share in the excitement that had inspired them. She was on the right track. All her forebodings forgotten, she pulled the chair from under the desk – Leonora's chair, where she had sat for hours writing the books for which she would long be remembered – and settled down to read more. When she came to the entry for the day before the discovery of Leonora's body, she exclaimed aloud in triumph.

'I knew it! Eat your heart out, DI Hollowhead! You'll have to listen to me now.'

For several seconds she sat re-reading the words that confirmed Ken Harris's misgivings and bore out everything that she, Iris and Bruce had subsequently conjectured. Gerard Hood *had* firmly scotched the notion of using mulberry tissue to disguise a valuable painting. Leonora had recorded her disappointment, but apparently accepted his verdict. She had then visited Arnie in his studio – *'a very strange young man with compelling eyes – but such talent!'*, she had written. It appeared that she had chatted to him quite freely about her own work as well as his, and he had responded by spontaneously taking the finished canvas from the easel and dumbly presenting it to her. She had, it seemed, demurred, but he had been insistent to the point of becoming agitated and so she had accepted and brought the picture home.

It was the final entry that seemed to clinch the matter once and for all:

'That unpleasant assistant of Gerard Hood's actually had the impertinence to telephone and demand that I return the picture. I informed her, politely but firmly, that it had

been a gift from the artist and that I had no intention of
wounding his feelings by parting with it. She spoke a great
deal of nonsense about its value to AFTER – such a foolish
acronym – and so I offered to donate its value to their
fund, but even that did not satisfy the tiresome creature.
In the end, I made it quite plain that if she argued any
further, she would get nothing at all.'

So that was it. Leonora had refused to part with the picture and
someone – Gerard Hood? – had taken it from her by force, and
with it, her life. Perhaps she had recognised the thief, or died
accidentally in the struggle . . . or, more probably, the intention
all along had been to kill her to prevent her reporting the theft
and the events preceding it. The key to her death had lain here
all these weeks.

Leonora's old-fashioned script, freely decorated with elaborate
flourishes, had not been easy to decipher. In order to give her
eyes a rest, Melissa raised her head to look out of the window.
As she did so, she glimpsed a momentary movement as
something black flashed past. Sensing that it had been a
reflection from the window behind her, she got up to look out at
the front garden, but there was nothing there. Probably a low-
flying bird, she thought to herself as she slipped the diary into
her pocket and felt for the keys. A blackbird possibly, or a crow.
Or maybe a magpie. The bird of ill-omen. One for sorrow . . .
Unaccountably, the sense of unease returned.

'Don't be a fool!' she muttered. She pushed the chair back
under the desk and from habit glanced round to make sure she
had left nothing behind. She realised with a jolt that her
handbag was still in the car . . . which was unlocked. There
had seemed no need for security in this deserted spot. But
one never knew who might be prowling around. Maybe that had
been unwise.

She hurried along the passage and out of the front door. As she turned to lock it, a black clad figure seemed to rise out of the ground before her. Eyes glittered through slits in a black hood. Black-gloved hands reached out and closed round her throat.

The pressure on her windpipe was murderous, her lungs screamed for air, red lights flashed before her eyes and there was a roaring in her ears. In an effort to break her assailant's grip, she tugged, frantically but uselessly, at his wrists. Helpless as a rag doll, she felt herself on the point of losing consciousness when advice she had once been given by Ken Harris swam into her blurred brain: 'If a man ever attacks you, Mel, don't hesitate – go straight for the nuts!'

She was still on her feet. With all the strength she had left, she raised her right knee and aimed for the groin. There was an outraged grunt and an oath, but the hands remained clamped round her throat. Their grip, however, momentarily slackened . . . just enough to enable her to draw a quick, strangled breath that half-inflated her collapsing lungs and gave her precious seconds to try again. This time, it was her hands that went for the target, clawing, gripping, twisting, squeezing. There was an animal yelp of pain; once more the grip round her throat eased as her assailant buckled at the knees. She threw her weight forward against him, kicking him on the ankle to throw him off balance. He went down, moaning in pain, almost dragging her with him, but releasing his hold just before he fell. There was a thud as the back of his head struck the stone step.

For several seconds, Melissa could do nothing but take deep, gasping breaths. She felt as if she could never draw enough air into her lungs to compensate for those terrible moments when she had been so near to suffocation. The man lay at her feet, not moving. Supposing he was dead? That would mean she had killed him. Was he still breathing? She bent down and pulled off the black woollen helmet that masked his head.

He was, she judged, in his late fifties, with a grizzled beard and thinning hair. She was on the point of trying to find out if he was still breathing, then changed her mind and stepped sharply out of reach of the outflung hands. He might be foxing, waiting for another chance to grab her. Even as the thought occurred to her, he gave a feeble groan and opened his eyes.

That was enough. He was still alive and coming round; at any moment he might be back on his feet. Melissa turned and fled, thankful that her car was pointing the right way, that it was unlocked with the key in the ignition . . . just what the police are always advising us not to do, she thought wryly, as she started the engine and sent the Golf tearing along the stony track towards the main road. Glancing in her mirror, she saw the man stagger to his feet and take a few lurching steps after her; she had not left a moment too soon.

The shock was beginning to tell. By the time she reached the village pub, where she knew there was a public telephone, she was trembling so violently that it took her several minutes to recover sufficiently to get out of the car. The parking area was behind the building, partially hidden from the road. The man probably had a car concealed somewhere; if he came after her, he would not see the Golf where she had left it, but he might very well guess that she would be here and come looking for her. She had taken off his mask; he would realise that she could identify him and be desperate to silence her. In a fit of panic, she broke into a run and almost fell through the door into the vestibule. The telephone was on the wall and there was no one using it. With a shaking hand, still keeping a fearful eye on the door, she lifted the receiver and tapped out 999.

While she was waiting for the police to arrive, she went into the bar and ordered coffee. A motherly-looking barmaid looked at her with a concerned expression.

'You okay, my love?' she asked, as she took the jug from its hotplate. 'You look as if you could use something stronger.' She hesitated for a moment before starting to pour, as if expecting Melissa to change her mind. It was tempting, but to tell her story with alcohol on her breath might convey the wrong impression . . . and there was the drive home . . .

'Coffee will be fine,' she assured the woman, with an attempt at a smile.

It was hot and fragrant, and she could feel it putting new life into her. She sat in a window seat where she could see everyone approaching the door . . . to watch for the patrol car that the woman on the emergency desk had promised, she told herself, but in reality keeping on the alert in case her attacker appeared. The police would want a description. She tried to conjure up a picture of his face as he lay unconscious at her feet. When she relived the moment when his eyes opened and stared up at her, she began to tremble again and almost spilt her coffee. There had been something about him . . . something almost familiar . . . and yet she was certain she had never seen him before.

The minutes ticked away. It was gone mid-day and a few people were coming in for a lunch-time drink and a sandwich. Melissa had eaten nothing since her early breakfast; she was starting to feel empty and went back to the bar for a bag of crisps, still keeping a wary eye on everyone who came in.

She heard the wail of a siren and a police car tore past with its blue light flashing, followed shortly afterwards by another, which turned into the forecourt and pulled up. She slipped outside and ran to meet it as Sergeant Waters got out. Her relief at the sight of a familiar face was overwhelming.

He opened a rear door, saying, 'Jump in.' She obeyed, and he got in beside her. 'Are you hurt?' he asked anxiously.

'My neck feels a bit stiff, that's all.' She put a hand to it as she spoke. It was the first time she had been aware of the discomfort; it brought the ghastly encounter all too vividly to mind and for a moment she feared she was going to puke. She hastily wound down the window and took several deep breaths.

'Let me see those marks,' said Waters when she had pulled herself together. She saw his expression change as he inspected her throat. 'We'll get a doctor to have a look at you when we get back to the station. How do you feel about going back to Quarry Cottage? It would help if you gave us your version of what happened on the spot.'

'No problem. I'm fine now.'

Looking back over the events of the next hour it seemed to Melissa that they had all been telescoped into a few minutes. When they reached their destination, the place was already alive with police. Two cars were parked close to the drive leading down to Quarry Cottage and a constable stood guarding the entrance. Another was stringing up yards of blue and white tape; by the front door, a third was speaking on his radio.

'Calling for a dog handler, Sarge,' he informed Waters. 'Traces of blood on the step, and we found this in a rose bush.' He held up the woollen hood which Melissa had snatched from her attacker's head; she must have tossed it aside as she sprinted for the car.

'Good. We'll let the dog get a sniff at that. Then bag it up for forensics.' Waters turned back to Melissa. 'I don't suppose you've any idea which direction he might have taken?'

'There's a footpath running past the cottage garden – it leads to a lane at the bottom of the hill. He might have gone that way.'

'You didn't see or hear a car?'

'No.'

The two officers conferred briefly; Melissa overheard a reference to 'the SS'; from her experience of police-speak, she guessed they were talking about the Sex Strangler. She shuddered at the realisation of what might have happened

186

to her. Another thought followed almost immediately: something didn't quite add up. It had to do with something someone had said . . . what was it? It was like a scrap of quicksilver rolling around in her mind, elusive, slipping away each time she tried to lay hold of it.

Presently they returned to police headquarters, stopping on the way to pick up Melissa's Golf which, despite her protests, Sergeant Waters insisted on driving himself. 'Not until you've seen the doctor,' he said firmly.

The doctor, a kindly soul, assured her that no serious damage had been done, but asked if she would mind having her bruises photographed. After that, someone brought her a cup of tea before she was taken to a room where a young officer manipulating a computer keyboard conjured up faces on a screen, patiently making changes until, with an inward shudder, she found herself looking at the likeness of her attacker.

'That him?' asked the officer.

She nodded, biting her lip. 'It's pretty close. I only looked at him for a few seconds. When he started to come round, I bolted.'

'Don't blame you.' He pressed some keys and a printer disgorged a sheet of paper, which he handed to her. 'Ever seen him before?'

'No, never, but . . .'

'But?' he prompted.

'There is something familiar about him. I think he reminds me of someone, but I can't think who . . .'

'Let us know if it comes to you, okay?'

'Of course.'

He escorted her to an interview room where she made her formal statement to Sergeant Waters. When she had told him everything she could remember, he went out; a few moments later a woman officer came in and sat down beside her.

'I'm WPC Mary Simmonds,' she said, in the manner of a

nurse reassuring an anxious patient. 'I've just popped in to ask if there's anything you want to add to your statement . . . anything you didn't feel like saying in front of Sergeant Waters?'

It took a moment for her meaning to sink in. Then Melissa said quickly, 'Oh, no, there was nothing like that. I didn't even think of it. I just thought he was trying to kill me.' Involuntarily, she put a hand to her throat, still painful after that awful, suffocating pressure.

'You're quite certain?' the woman persisted gently. 'It's very important that you tell us everything.'

'If he had any ideas in that direction – and I don't think he did – he's in no state to follow them up at the moment, not after what I did to him.' Melissa gave an involuntary chuckle; the flash of black humour had done a lot to relieve the tension. WPC Simmonds smiled, wrote something in her notebook and stood up.

'Good for you,' she said. 'That'll be all for now. We'll just get you to sign your statement before you leave. Are you fit to drive home? Do you think you should see your own doctor?'

'I'm fine, thank you.' Melissa's one desire now was to be by herself, to think. She had a growing conviction that a vital clue was within her grasp, but it would not reveal itself. She was still groping in the dark.

Chapter Twenty-Two

Melissa went back to her car, fumbled in her handbag for the key and found herself holding instead the keys to Quarry Cottage. Someone – she could not remember who – had found them on the ground and handed them to her. Sergeant Waters had asked how she came to be at the cottage and she had explained, without elaboration, that she had gone there to pick up Leonora's diary. Knowing that she was writing the final chapters of *Deadly Legacy*, he had accepted her reason for wanting to retrieve it as perfectly natural. There had been no suggestion that it had any connection with what was evidently being treated as a random attack by a dangerous psychopath. And in the shock and confusion, she had not thought to raise the possibility. All the police questions had been concerned with the attack itself, all their efforts directed towards catching the perpetrator, and until now the same thought had been uppermost in her own, somewhat dazed mind.

She patted the pocket of her anorak to check that the diary was still there, telling herself that she really ought to go back into the police station, ask to speak to someone about the enquiry into Leonora's death – that probably meant Detective Inspector Holloway, she thought with a grimace – and tell him everything she knew.

Everything? That would entail admitting her part in the break-in at Blackwater Hall, because the diary entries in themselves contained nothing incriminating. There would, of course, be the fact that no picture by Arnie Barron had been found in Quarry Cottage, but without evidence to the contrary, it would be assumed that the thief had made off with it, along with the handful of other items and the contents of Leonora's handbag, in the hope that it might fetch the price of a few snorts of cocaine. It was easy to imagine an expression of condescension and disbelief spreading over DI Holloway's features as she tried to convince him that it concealed something of far greater value. She simply couldn't face it, not now, not after what she had just been through. Besides, it would be sensible to check with Bruce first, to see if he had discovered anything further that would lend weight to their story.

Bruce. He was supposed to be handing over to the police the photographs of the Boudin painting the two of them had discovered in Gerard Hood's flat. He had something else on his mind as well, something that occurred to him the previous evening, but which he had refused to discuss then and there because it might be 'just a red herring'. It was time to find out how things stood – but first, the keys had to be returned to Mr Semple's office.

Again, Melissa hesitated. After what she had told him on the telephone, the solicitor would certainly want to know if the diary contained anything to support her theory. She quailed at the prospect of more questions; she would pretend that she hadn't yet read it and would promise to let him know if there was anything worth following up. Mr Semple seemed a reasonable man; he'd be sure to understand. She got into the car and headed for the town centre.

When the entered the offices of Rathbone and Semple, there was no one in reception. She was tempted to leave the keys on the desk and slip out unobserved, but just as she was pulling them from her handbag, Miss Gudgeon appeared with an armful of folders. She stopped short at the sight of Melissa and her jaw dropped. For a moment, she appeared dumbfounded.

'Is something wrong?' Melissa asked.

'Mrs Craig! That's what I was going to ask you.' For once, the secretary's air of detachment appeared shaken, allowing genuine concern to break through. 'Whatever has happened? You look quite ill.'

Melissa realised with a start that she had not given her appearance a thought, or so much as combed her hair, since the attack. 'Goodness, I must look an absolute fright!' she exclaimed. 'I've had a rather nasty experience . . . a man grabbed me as I was leaving the cottage, but I'm all right now . . .'

'Grabbed you? How awful! Are you hurt?'

'No, just a bit shocked. I've reported it to the police and they're investigating. May I use your loo to tidy myself up?'

'Of course. It's along there.' Miss Gudgeon half turned to indicate a passage behind her. 'Can I get you anything? Some tea or coffee perhaps?'

'No, thank you. I just came in to return the key.'

In the ladies' room, Melissa washed her face and hands and ran a comb through her ruffled hair. She studied her pale, drawn features in the mirror; she did indeed look awful. Thank goodness Ken can't see me now, she thought. What I need more than anything is a good rest . . . and time to think.

When she got back to reception, Miss Gudgeon was on the telephone. As Melissa approached, she ended her call and put the instrument down. 'I was trying to contact Mr Semple, but he's not available,' she explained. 'He'll be so upset to hear of your dreadful experience.'

'Tell him I'll be in touch later,' said Melissa. 'I'll leave these with you.' She handed over the keys, politely declined a further offer of tea or coffee, and left. She had had enough of solicitude; all she wanted was to go home.

Back in Hawthorn Cottage, she downed a stiff gin and tonic, ate a cheese sandwich and began to feel better. She called Bruce's office, but he was out. She wished Iris wasn't away. If Iris knew what had happened to her that morning, she would insist on putting her through a routine of calming yoga exercises. A very good idea, Melissa thought. She changed into leggings and a sweatshirt and spent an hour in what Iris called 'deep relaxation', flat on her back on the sitting-room floor.

When she got up she felt almost restored, apart from the discomfort in her neck and throat. The collar of her anorak had afforded some protection, but even so there were livid marks on her neck. She examined them in the bathroom mirror and the horror of the experience returned to set her stomach churning. She thought of Simon, who had so nearly become an orphan, and then of Ken Harris, lying in his hospital bed, confident that her work on Leonora's unfinished book would 'keep her out of mischief'. At least, she thought, this particular adventure could have happened to anyone. She had just been in the wrong place at the wrong time.

But was that really the case? Back came the nagging feeling that something had been overlooked. With her hand still gently massaging her neck, she remembered what Bruce had told her in confidence about the investigation into Carole's murder. There had been discrepancies between the marks on her throat and those on the previous victims of the so-called Sex Strangler. *They* had not died, and the signs were that murder had never been the motive for the attacks on them. The pressure on the throat had been calculated to render unconscious, not to kill.

Iris had spoken of having 'a funny feeling' about the death of Carole Prescot. Supposing it was Carole's killer who had carried out the attack on Melissa as well? She was already convinced that the objective had not been indecent assault, but murder. It might, of course, have been the work of some copy-cat pervert with homicidal leanings, who had been prowling in the neighbourhood and spotted her as an easy target. That seemed to be the line the police were taking. But supposing she had been the intended victim all along? Had the motive been to stop her revealing the contents of the diary? In that case, her attacker must have been aware of its existence and importance – and of the fact that she was going to Quarry Cottage that morning to collect it. Someone had told him, but who besides herself knew?

There was Jonathan Round. After an initial reluctance to co-operate, he had been reasonably helpful – but that might have been a blind. Her telephone call about the diary might have caught him off guard, leaving him with no way of refusing her request to hunt for his godmother's diary without arousing suspicion.

Mr Semple, of course, knew of her proposed visit to Quarry Cottage because he had given Miss Gudgeon permission to hand over the keys. Finally, there was Miss Gudgeon herself. She had made every possible excuse not to part with the keys. Perhaps that had been a delaying tactic. Realising that she was dealing with someone not easily put off, and that she would certainly be instructed to hand them over, she could have alerted the unknown assailant and let him know when and where to find Melissa. It could explain why she had looked so shaken when Melissa appeared, dishevelled but alive and unharmed, in the office.

Carole had spoken of a discovery that 'might be important'. Perhaps she had already mentioned it to her colleague, not realising that she had unwittingly stumbled on some irregularity which, if brought to their employer's notice, might lead to unwelcome enquiries. If Miss Gudgeon *was* in some way involved, and had overheard Carole's telephone call to Melissa, she might have feared exposure.

Exposure of what? The goings-on at Blackwater Hall? Surely

not. What connection could there be between Miss Gudgeon and a ring of art thieves? It did not take long for a name to bob up in Melissa's head: Gerard Hood, the man at the centre of the scam, the womaniser whose affairs were said to be the cause of disagreements between him and his regular partner, Eloise Dampier. As secretary to one of Cheltenham's most prominent solicitors, Miss Gudgeon could well have access to information about valuable art treasures owned by some of his wealthy clients – information that could be of great interest to Hood. But *was* she involved with him? Melissa had no means of finding out. In any case, would she have been prepared to act as his informant, even if it made her an accessory to murder?

At this point in her reasoning, Melissa, who had been prowling from room to room in her agitation, stopped short, feeling as if a lump of lead had landed in the pit of her stomach. One way or the other, there was a strong probability that Gerard Hood knew she had the diary and might at this very moment be studying it. Miss Gudgeon claimed to have been trying to contact Mr Semple while Melissa was in the ladies' room, but it could just as easily have been Hood. Bruce suspected him of being Leonora's killer . . . but it was certainly not Hood who had tried to throttle Melissa. The situation was becoming more complex by the minute.

Next came a far more chilling thought. What if the assassin were to track her down here, to finish what he had failed to do at the first attempt? Her address was on the business card she had given to Miss Gudgeon. Close to panic, she rushed round the cottage, checking that the doors and windows were secure, peering nervously outside into the gathering dusk before drawing the curtains. She felt like an animal that had gone to ground and was waiting, trembling, for a ruthless pursuer.

The sound of the telephone made her jump. But the voice of the caller brought immediate reassurance.

'Oh, Mr Semple!' she exclaimed, 'I'm so glad to hear from you!'

'My dear Mrs Craig, Miss Gudgeon has told me of your ordeal. You sound terribly shaken, and no wonder.' His friendly concern, so different from his dignified professional manner, almost brought tears to Melissa's eyes.

'It was pretty awful,' she replied. 'I was feeling a whole lot better, but now . . .' She broke off, uncertain what to say next, hesitating to blurt out there and then her suspicion that his secretary might be involved in a serious crime.

'Has something else happened?' he asked.

'Not exactly, but I've been reading Leonora's diary.'

'You've discovered something about that matter you were speaking of earlier?'

'Yes . . . no, that is, it's more than that . . . Oh dear, I don't know where to begin.'

'I take it you've told the police about it?'

'I haven't told anyone yet . . . at least, I told the police everything I could remember about the attack, of course, but something else has just occurred to me, something I think you should know first.'

Suddenly, her course became clear. She would tell him the whole story from start to finish including the adventure at Blackwater Hall. If she ever found herself on a charge of breaking and entering, she would need legal advice anyway. With his long experience of appraising a situation from an objective standpoint, he was exactly the person to turn to. Why on earth hadn't she thought of it before?

She heard him saying, 'Do you want to tell me about it?' and she replied earnestly, 'That's exactly what I want, but not on the telephone. It's very complicated . . . and a bit delicate . . . someone may be listening in.'

If he found the idea surprising, he betrayed no sign, merely saying, 'Would you like to come to my office? I have no further appointments this afternoon – we can talk in complete privacy.'

'Yes, please . . . no, I can't, I daren't leave the house.' At the thought of who might be lurking outside, all her terrors returned.

'I *quite* understand,' he said earnestly. 'In that case, I'll call on you, if that's convenient.'

'I'd be grateful if you would. I'm on my own here and my neighbour's away . . .'

He tut-tutted sympathetically. 'Not the best situation after your ordeal,' he said kindly. 'I have one or two matters to attend to here and then I'll come straight to your house.'

'It's very good of you.'

'Not at all. In a way, I feel responsible for what has happened. After all, Miss Jewell was my client, and if you hadn't been so conscientious about completing her work, you would never have had such a terrible experience.'

'I really do appreciate it.' She gave him directions to Hawthorn Cottage and put down the phone, almost dizzy with relief. Catching sight of herself in the hall mirror, she decided that her exercise gear was too casual for receiving a visit from a solicitor, and went upstairs to change into something more suitable.

Chapter Twenty-Three

Mr Semple seemed to be a very long time arriving. Unable to settle, constantly listening for his car, Melissa found herself drawing aside the curtains every few minutes to look out, imagining she had heard a sound. The porch light illuminated the front drive, but left in darkness the approach by the valley footpath. From that direction anyone could sneak up unobserved. How many times had Ken Harris expressed reservations about her living in such an isolated spot? She had always dismissed his fears; now she was sharing them a thousandfold. Was there someone lurking out there even now, preparing to smash his way in and finish off what he had failed to do earlier? 'Oh, Mr Semple, where are you?' she exclaimed aloud. 'Please, *please* get here soon.'

When she heard the crunch of wheels on the gravel, she flew to the sitting-room window to make sure it was him. Her relief at the sight of him getting out of the car was indescribable. She hurried to the door and opened it before he had time to ring the bell.

'I'm so thankful you're here,' she said shakily as she led the way to the sitting-room. 'I've been getting really jumpy, thinking that awful man might come bursting in at any moment.'

He gave a sympathetic nod. 'I quite understand your feeling nervous, but I understood the attack on you was purely a random one. What makes you suppose . . . ?'

'I don't believe it was random,' she broke in. 'I believe I was singled out, because of what I've discovered. That's why I'm feeling so scared, but at least he won't try anything while you're here.'

But he may, after you've gone. The unspoken fear made her turn cold again. Her thoughts ran on: *I'll have to go to a hotel for the night, I can't stay here alone, I'll leave when Mr Semple goes . . .*

'Well now, aren't you going to ask me to sit down?' The solicitor's friendly voice brought her back from the edge of hysteria.

'Of course, please forgive me.'

'How very cosy this is,' he commented as he settled into the armchair opposite hers. His approving glance took in the low ceiling with its exposed beams, the bookshelves on either side of the chimney-breast, the log fire on the stone hearth. 'This place is quite a gem, Mrs Craig. How long have you lived here?'

'Getting on for four years.'

'And these are all your books?' He glanced up at the array of similar bindings that filled two of the shelves, then turned back to Melissa. 'Quite a prodigious output,' he said, evidently impressed. 'Not quite equal to poor Miss Jewell's, of course, but . . .'

'Well, I am quite a big younger,' she pointed out, 'so I've got plenty of time to catch up.'

'Quite so.' He cleared his throat. 'Before we begin, Mrs Craig, would you mind telling me which member of my staff you suspected might be listening to our conversation on the telephone?'

Melissa hesitated, then said, 'Miss Gudgeon. It may sound ridiculous,' she added, as his initial expression of astonishment gave way to a shake of the head and an incredulous smile, 'but I really believe she's involved with some very dangerous people.

I'll come to that later, if you don't mind. There's a great deal more to tell you first. I'll begin with this.' She picked up Leonora's diary, which lay on a side table at her elbow, opened it at the final entry and handed it to him.

He studied the page for several seconds, frowning and gnawing his lower lip. 'This reference to a picture – is this strange young man Miss Jewell refers to a famous artist, then?'

'Oh no, but I believe that particular picture was very valuable. So valuable that someone was prepared to commit murder to recover it.'

'I don't follow you . . .'

'I think you will when you've heard the whole story. That entry confirms what I've suspected all along. I'll try and tell you everything in the order it happened, but please forgive me if things get a bit out of sequence.'

'Just take your time.' He crossed his legs, folded his hands against his stomach and cocked his head a little to one side.

'It all began when a business card from an art gallery in Gloucester Docks fell out of Leonora's research notes,' she began. 'I had the feeling that she'd intended to make some changes to the ending of *Deadly Legacy*, but I couldn't find any details. So I went to see a man called Sam Deacon, whose name was on the card, and made some enquiries. He confirmed that Leonora had been to see him, and referred me to Gerard Hood, the curator of the Asser Foundation collection at Blackwater Hall.'

As concisely as possible, she recounted the story from the beginning: her first visit to Blackwater Hall with Bruce and Iris, the bizarre encounter with Arnie Barron, Iris's suspicions about the blank prepared canvas that had so agitated Eloise Dampier and the discovery that Gerard Hood purchased mulberry tissue for purposes other than the restoration of old paintings. Mr Semple listened without interrupting, his eyes fixed on the glowing logs.

'It was Iris who twigged what he was using it for,' Melissa explained, 'but of course, it was only guesswork. We wanted to find out whether she was right. If she was, it seemed to point to Leonora's death being murder, not an accident. I think I mentioned this to you on the telephone.'

'You did. You also hinted that *that*' – he pointed to the diary – 'might contain something to confirm your suspicions. You've said nothing to the police?'

'I tried several times to contact Detective Chief Inspector Harris, but he wasn't answering his phone. I left a message, asking him to call back, but he didn't. And then we – Iris and I – heard about Carole Prescot being murdered.'

'Ah, yes, poor Carole. A dreadful business.' Mr Semple shook his head in sorrow at the recollection. Then he gave Melissa a keen look. 'Are you suggesting there's a connection?'

'I believe there is, but I didn't suspect it at the time, none of us did. Perhaps I could leave that for the moment?'

He raised a hand in a gesture of agreement. 'Forgive the interruption. Please continue.'

'Carole phoned me a day or two before her death, wanting to meet me,' Melissa continued. 'She never said what it was about, but when I saw the news of the murder on television, I went to the police to report it, just in case it might be important. That was when I learned that DCI Harris was seriously ill.'

'And you still omitted to tell the police about the . . . what did you call it? Mulberry tissue?'

'Yes, but not intentionally, it genuinely slipped my mind. Ken Harris is a friend of mine and I was upset to know how ill he was. And later, when I thought about it, I realised I'd have to deal with Inspector Holloway again, and I was sure he wouldn't take me seriously. I'd had a brush with him already about that piece of angle iron that I found. Did you hear, by the way, that it disappeared before the police got to it?'

'Yes, I heard.' Mr Semple gave an odd little smile and she wondered if he too might have had some contact with the self-opinionated DI Holloway during his dealings with the police. 'Please go on with your story, Mrs Craig.'

'I'm afraid you're not going to approve of the next bit.'

'Allow me to be the judge of that.'

Melissa took a deep breath before explaining how she had confided Iris's theory to Bruce, the subsequent escapade at Blackwater Hall the previous evening and the discovery of the Boudin painting in Gerard Hood's flat. As her narrative proceeded she saw a series of changes in the solicitor's expression. Apprehension was followed in rapid succession by astonishment, disbelief and alarm. When she had finished, he slapped the arms of his chair in a gesture of outrage and then sat for several minutes, staring into the fire with his mouth set in a hard line, saying nothing. When, finally, he turned to look her full in the face, she quailed before the anger in his eyes.

'Please, don't be too cross with me,' she pleaded. 'I don't expect a pat on the back for what we did, but at least give me your advice. It will all have to come out, of course – Bruce will have been to the police by now . . .'

'*What* did you say?' She saw his knuckles turn white as his hands tightened their grip on the chair. 'I thought you said the police knew nothing of this.'

'Bruce took some photos of the Boudin and he was going to show them to the police and tell them . . . Mr Semple, are you all right? You've gone quite pale. Can I get you a drink?'

'I'm afraid it will take more than a drink to undo the damage that you and your meddling friends have done,' he said, in a voice thick with fury. His features, drained of colour, were distorted and almost unrecognisable; all trace of professional composure had disappeared.

It took Melissa a second or two to grasp the appalling nature of the mistake she had made. Her heart seemed to stop; her hand flew to her mouth.

'*You*!' she exclaimed in a hoarse whisper. 'You're in the scam as well!'

'Not just *in* it.' He straightened in his chair and raised his head. 'The entire plan was my idea,' he informed her proudly, 'and under my direction it has run like clockwork.'

'So it was you who gave orders for me to be killed . . . and Leonora?'

'Of course.' He had quickly recovered his sangfroid. 'We couldn't have foolish women endangering our very lucrative arrangement.'

'What about Carole?' faltered Melissa, feeling a fresh stab of horror. 'Did you . . . ?'

'Yes, it was a pity about Carole.' An independent observer, knowing nothing of the circumstances, would have sworn the man felt genuine regret. 'Such a conscientious employee,' he sighed. 'Too conscientious for her own good, I'm afraid. She sacrificed her life to save me the cost of a telephone call. Ironic, isn't it?'

'A telephone call?' For an instant, Melissa forgot her own danger in her attempt to understand.

'One of her duties was to check my cellphone account,' Mr Semple explained. 'I overlooked, when I passed it to her . . .'

'That it contains details, including the time, of every call you make!' Melissa burst out. 'Oh, why didn't I spot that at the time? Your battery was never flat, you never attempted to call the police while we were in the Ploughman's Arms. You called your accomplice, and you wanted to give him time to retrieve the weapon that killed Leonora Jewell. And then you made the mistake of calling your secretary, to tell her to have a form of receipt ready for me to sign . . . and later, when Carole came to check the account, she realised it didn't tally with what you'd told the police, she knew you'd been lying to them . . .'

'Oh, no!' Mr Semple appeared mildly shocked. 'She quite properly came straight to me to point out the discrepancy. I told her it was a mistake and I'd take it up with Vodafone. I thought I'd set her mind at rest, but when I heard her speaking to you it was obvious she had given the matter further thought. I decided it was too risky to allow her to voice her suspicions to anyone else.'

'So you had her murdered.' Melissa felt a wave of loathing at the cold-bloodedness of the man. 'You . . . you monster!'

He looked wounded. 'I prefer "silenced",' he said reproachfully. 'It was unfortunate, I admit, but as I said, I was not prepared to allow a foolish young woman to destroy everything I had worked for. That reminds me,' he added, almost as an aside to an invisible secretary, 'something will have to be done about the Dampier woman. Hood tells me she could be a danger to us as well.'

'Haven't you done enough killing?' For the moment, Melissa's anger overcame her fear. 'Just for a few miserable pictures.'

'*Miserable* pictures? My dear Mrs Craig, it is plain you have no appreciation of works of art, or of the wealth that they represent. My partners and I have been, shall we say, providing for a very comfortable early retirement. I'm afraid it will have to be earlier than we planned, thanks to your interference. The immediate problem is, what are we going to do with you?'

'You can't kill me now. You're sure to be caught,' said Melissa desperately. 'If you know what's good for you, you'll give yourself up.'

'Give myself up?' He was actually smiling, looking for all the world like the respectable family solicitor she had believed him to be. 'You underestimate me, Mrs Craig. You are quite right, though, it would be rather short-sighted to kill you now. In fact, you will be much more valuable to us alive.'

'What do you mean?' Melissa's mouth had become so dry and stiff that she could barely get the words out. 'What are you going to do?'

He glanced at his watch. 'Well now, my good friend Tom is waiting not far away for a call from me.'

'Tom? Tom Barron?' Now she knew why the man's face had been familiar. He was the father of Arnie, the man whom she and Bruce suspected of masterminding the burglaries that provided Hood with the material for his 'mulberry sandwiches'. The pieces of the puzzle were finally slotting into place. Too late, she thought despairingly.

'Tom Barron is a valuable member of our organisation,' said Semple. 'The plan this evening was that I should establish exactly how much you knew and then for him to finish what he unfortunately failed to do this morning. I'm afraid the arrangements will have to be altered now. He'll be very upset about it; he was hoping to avenge that rather painful injury you inflicted on him.'

'I wish I'd bloody well crippled him!' Melissa snarled.

'Such unladylike language!' Mr Semple shook his head in reproof. 'Let me see, now. A trip with Tom to somewhere safe and secure will be the answer, I think. It may be a little uncomfortable for you, but it shouldn't be for too long. We'll set a price for your safe return . . . it will be interesting to establish how much you are worth to your friends. Perhaps your publishers will consider making a contribution? In the meantime . . .' He took out his cellphone and punched in a number.

'I'm not going anywhere with you!' While he was occupied with his call, she looked frantically around for some means of escape. Her eye fell on the poker lying on the hearth. It was out of her reach, but if she moved quickly enough . . . she made a dive, but he had followed her gaze and anticipated the movement.

Dropping the phone, he snatched up the poker before she could reach it and raised it above his shoulder.

'Sit down!' he commanded harshly. 'Any more tricks and I'll break your arm.' He brandished the heavy metal bar inches from her face. Half mesmerised with terror, she sank back into her chair. 'That's better. Just do exactly as I tell you from now on. Provided your friends do the same, no harm will come to you.'

After what seemed an eternity, during which he remained standing over her with the poker in his hand, there came the sound of footsteps approaching the cottage. Moment later, the doorbell rang. 'Answer that?' he ordered.

She could do nothing but obey. Even had he left her alone for the few seconds it would take him to go to the front door himself, every window in the room was locked – she had secured them herself and could never get one open in time. There was no way out. On legs that threatened to collapse beneath her, she stumbled into the hall with her captor at her heels. With shaking hands, she opened the door.

In the porch, with two burly figures behind him, stood Detective Inspector Desmond Holloway.

Chapter Twenty-Four

It was over in seconds. Charles Semple, in a futile attempt to avoid arrest, made a grab at Melissa from behind, threatened to brain her – and anyone else who tried to block his way – with the poker, and was disarmed with almost nonchalant ease by Holloway's two hefty companions. Melissa would long remember the look of hatred he gave her as he was led away.

WPC Simmonds materialised from nowhere and took Melissa by the arm. 'You're not hurt?' she asked anxiously.

'No, I'm fine . . . but I could use a drink.'

'Let me get it for you.'

'In the kitchen.'

'Call me Mary,' said the policewoman as, following Melissa's directions, she found the brandy and poured some into a glass. 'Don't go knocking it back in one go,' she warned as she handed it over.

Melissa, who had tottered rather than walked to a chair at the kitchen table, gave a wan smile and sipped obediently. She was too shaken to resent being ordered about in her own home.

There was a step outside, and the sound of the front door closing. 'That'll be Detective Inspector Holloway,' said Mary. She popped her head round the door and called, 'In here, sir.'

He entered the room and sat down opposite Melissa without waiting to be asked. 'Any chance of some tea?' he said.

'Go ahead,' said Melissa in response to Mary's look of enquiry.

'You'll find everything in that cupboard. There's milk in the fridge.'

'I imagine you're wondering how we came to arrive at such an opportune moment?' There was more than a hint of complacency in Holloway's manner.

Melissa, her nerve restored as much by the knowledge that her principal enemy was under lock and key as by the brandy, gave him a cool nod. 'It had occurred to me to ask,' she said. Then something clicked in her memory, and she added urgently, 'Tom Barron is lurking somewhere around . . . he's the one who . . .'

'We know all about Barron,' said Holloway smoothly. 'In fact, he directed us here.'

'What?' A short time ago, as she and Semple confronted one another in her sitting-room, everything had become clear. Now it was getting confused again.

'We've had our eye on Tom Barron for a while,' said Holloway. 'We've suspected him of certain illegal fringe activities connected with his second-hand car business –in fact, we've pulled him in once or twice for questioning, but we've never been able to make anything stick. He's not over-bright, but he's a wily bird and he asks for the same legal adviser who gets him off the hook each time: Charles Semple.'

'Ah!' That was something she hadn't thought of.

'Nothing sinister in that, of course,' Holloway continued, 'until we tumbled to the fact that Semple had also been present when we were questioning another suspect, someone we thought might be the so-called Sex Strangler. During that interview, certain details were mentioned about the Strangler's methods that have never been made public.'

'And those details were passed on, so that Carole Prescot's murder could be made to look like the Strangler's handiwork!' exclaimed Melissa. 'I wonder if that's what B . . .' In the nick of

208

time, she checked herself from blurting out Bruce Ingram's name.

'That was almost certainly Barron's intention.' Holloway gave no sign of having noticed the slip she had so nearly made. 'As it happens, we weren't fooled, but we've been keeping quiet about that,' he went on. 'I've no doubt the idea was to repeat the process after killing you, but luckily you managed to escape.'

'And gave us that excellent likeness of Barron,' added Mary, as she brought three cups of tea and a bowl of sugar to the table, pulled up another chair and sat down.

'Quite.' Holloway looked far from pleased at the interruption. 'As it happens, there was even less chance of his getting away with it this time.'

'How was that?'

'We have the Strangler safely locked up in a police cell. He tried his tricks early this morning on a young lady whose hobbies are martial arts and weight-lifting. He's not feeling his best at the moment.' A rare smile flitted across Holloway's normally wooden features.

'Well, thank God for that!' Melissa exclaimed fervently. 'What I still don't understand is, where Tom Barron fitted into the set-up. I mean, it's obvious he was involved in the robberies, delivering the stolen paintings to Gerard Hood and so on . . . but murder! How come he agreed to that?'

'Semple appears to have had an extraordinary hold over everyone in his organisation. In Barron's case, having got him off some lesser charges in the past by some fancy legal footwork, it wasn't difficult to get him to carry out a few small services in return. Barron began by providing the getaway cars, then driving them, and he also passed on useful information about likely houses to target through dodgy contacts. As time went on, he got in deeper and deeper – and found the racket more and more lucrative – until he was prepared to do anything Semple told him, including killing Leonora Jewell to retrieve a picture his

209

son had given her. But that's another story,' the detective added, with an air of mystery that Melissa was tempted to puncture by informing him that she knew at least as much about it as he did, probably more. Sensibly, she refrained.

'There's no doubt Semple has a dominating personality,' she said. 'I wonder what made Barron confess everything so readily? He must have been singing like the proverbial canary.'

'He was still recovering from his, shall we say, encounter with you when we called, and wasn't exactly on top form. It came out later that he'd had a further call from Semple, informing him that as he'd bungled the job he, Semple that is, would be there next time to make sure it was done properly. By this time Barron was so shaken up by the whole business that he was on the point of going to pieces. He's admitted that he never bargained for murder – all he wants now is out. So you see,' Holloway finished, making a grandiloquent gesture with his mug of tea, 'we arrested him at psychologically the right moment.' The manner in which he made this pronouncement suggested that this superb piece of timing was due entirely to his own perspicacity.

His smirk faded when Melissa commented artlessly, 'What a bit of luck for you.'

'Er, yes, wasn't it,' he agreed, with evident reluctance.

Melissa was silent for a few minutes while she digested the new information. Then she said, 'Going back to Carole's murder, I assume you found out about the phone calls – the ones Semple made when his cellphone was supposed to have a flat battery?'

'Of course. You were of some help to us there,' Holloway said graciously.

Melissa, doing her best to hide her irritation, said coolly, 'I'm so glad.'

'On the face of it, your report about the call you received from Carole told us very little, but I sent one of my officers to make routine enquiries among the staff of Rathbone and Semple. We thought someone might have known – or guessed – why she wanted to speak to you. One of the employees recalled that she had seen Carole checking Semple's cellphone account and heard her say to herself, "That's not right". Then she took it into his office and came back without it. No one thought anything of it at the time; Semple himself brushed it aside as a computer error that he'd asked to have corrected, but I wasn't satisfied and got hold of a copy of the statement. Apart from showing that Semple *had* used the cellphone – to call Tom Barron and, of course, his own office – during the period he claimed the battery was flat, there were several other calls to Barron's number, some of them quite lengthy. The E-FIT likeness of your attacker, unmistakably Barron, seemed to clinch matters.'

With the air of a man whose important task has been irreproachably carried out, Holloway sat back and took copious swallows of tea.

'You haven't said how you knew Semple was here,' said Melissa.

'Easy.' He wiped his mouth with the back of his hand. 'Barron told us.'

'When?'

'About half an hour ago. As soon as we got him down to the station he asked for his brief. We told him he wasn't getting Semple and dropped some broad hints as to why. That seems to have been the last straw, that and the hope that things might go easier for him if he co-operated. We let him have his cellphone and we all waited for Semple's call. It was only then that Barron told us where to find him. We came as quickly as we could.' Once again, the smug smile made Melissa cringe as he went on, 'Barron will sing like a bird from now on. Gerard Hood and Eloise Dampier should have been picked up as well – it'll be interesting to hear what they have to say. Quite a good day's work all round.' He drained his teacup and, without taking his eyes from Melissa, held it out for Mary to refill.

'Congratulations,' said Melissa, trying to inject some warmth into her voice. She supposed she should thank him for coming to her rescue, but could not bring herself to do so. His air of self-satisfaction made the words stick in her throat.

Then something else occurred to her. 'If you knew all this beforehand, why didn't you arrest Semple before he came here and scared me half to death?' she demanded.

For the first time, she had him on the defensive. 'We had nothing concrete to link him with Barron except the fact that he'd advised him professionally on comparatively minor matters in the past,' he admitted. 'All we had on Barron when we picked him up was that he matched the E-FIT of your attacker. It wasn't until we got our hands on the cellphone account that we had the breakthrough. That arrived by special messenger at about six o'clock, by which time Semple had left his office. We confronted Barron with the account and that's when he really began to talk. He's now playing the hapless victim of an evil genius.' There was a pause before Holloway said, with only the merest hint of humility, 'I'm sorry you had such a traumatic experience.'

'It must have been terrible for you,' said Mary as, at a signal from her superior, she got up to leave. 'I think you've coped amazingly well. Are you sure you'll be all right now? I daresay I could stay . . . ?'

Her glance swivelled in Holloway's direction, but before he could respond Melissa said firmly, 'I'll be perfectly all right, but thanks for the offer.'

On the way to the door, Holloway said, almost as an afterthought, 'There are several things I'd like to ask *you*, Mrs Craig – when you're fully recovered from your ordeal, of course. I'm sure you'll be able to help us fill in a few details.' His expression was bland, but something in his voice told her he had guessed that she knew far more about the affair than she had so far revealed.

'Yes, of course,' she replied, her heart sinking a little. That the case could be tied up without her having to reveal her part in it had been too much to hope for.

After the two officers left she had a long, relaxing soak in a hot bath before calling Bruce at his home.

'I've only just got back,' he said. He sounded breathless. 'Things have been buzzing down at the nick – Tom Barron's been pulled in, and Gerard and Eloise . . . and now Charles Semple, who's turned out to be the big fish himself. *And* they've got the Strangler.'

'So what else is new?' asked Melissa. It was her turn to feel smug.

'You've heard all this?' He sounded incredulous. 'How, for heaven's sake?'

'Semple was arrested at my house, and I've had the insufferable DI Holloway here, preening himself on his cleverness.'

'What the hell was Semple doing in your house?'

'He'd arranged to meet Tom Barron here. Between them, they planned to bump me off. Then, when I let drop that by now the fuzz would know all about it, Charlie boy decided he was going to hold me hostage.'

'Good God!' Bruce sounded horrified. 'What happened? Are you hurt?'

'Not in the least. Instead of Tom Barron arriving to cart me off to some destination unknown, it was DI Knight-in-Shining-Armour-Holloway who came galloping to the rescue.'

'Was it now? And did he by any chance tell you what put him on to Semple?'

'He did. He reminded me of Little Jack Horner pulling out

plums. He'd spotted a link between Tom Barron and a man suspected of being the Sex Strangler. It seems . . .'

'They were both advised by that pillar of the legal establishment, Charles Semple,' Bruce interposed.

'That's right. How did you know?'

'Because I was the one who turned it up and fed him the information,' said Bruce.

'Was that what you were being so secretive about yesterday?'

'Right. It occurred to me as a possibility, but I didn't want to say anything until I was sure.'

'Well, good for you. You keep me in the dark while I entertain the villain of the piece and narrowly escape a fate worse then death . . . thanks very much.'

'I don't follow.'

She gave him a brief account of the circumstances that had led to Semple's visit to Hawthorn Cottage.

'Oh Melissa, I'm so sorry – it never entered my head that you'd spill the beans to him. You've had a hell of a day – are you sure you're all right?'

'I'm fine, and you can take your Brownie points. I doubt if you'll get much else in the way of credit. Hollowhead will keep that for himself.'

'Who cares, as long as you're okay and all the villains rounded up. How about meeting me for a drink to celebrate?'

Melissa glanced at the clock. It was barely half-past nine, but it suddenly dawned on her that she was utterly exhausted. 'Thanks, but no thanks,' she replied. 'All I want now is bed. Ken Harris is being transferred to Cheltenham tomorrow; if I turn up to visit him looking like I feel at the moment, he'll have a relapse on the spot. I've also got a book to finish.'

'Of course – *Deadly Legacy*. Now you'll be able to finish it the way Leonora intended.'

'So I shall.' The thought gave her enormous pleasure. 'When

it's published, I think I'll give a copy to Arnie. I'll tell him it's from the writing lady.'

'That's a nice idea. Will her picture be on the cover?'

'Sure to be. Bruce, what will become of Arnie now?'

'That's been worrying me. I'm sure the Pattersons will look after him, but he'll miss his studio at Blackwater Hall – and all the perks that went with it.'

'His paintings must have made quite a bit of money for the Asser Foundation. Maybe the new curator will let him carry on there.'

'Let's hope so. Well, Melissa, if you won't come out for a drink, I'll get on and write my story.'

'You do that,' she said, 'but please, leave my name out of it.'

The Benbury Barnstormers' Christmas show was voted the best ever by the enthusiastic audience. The script was the wittiest, the acting the most professional and the costumes the most original, but the greatest praise was reserved for the sets, designed by and executed under the professional guidance of Iris Ash.

After attending the first performance, Melissa and Iris, escorted respectively by Kenneth Harris and Jack Hammond, joined the cast and the backstage helpers in Benbury's only pub, the Woolpack. Presently, the four of them walked the short distance down the lane leading to Hawthorn and Elder Cottages, cosily hidden at the end of their secluded track. Ken had an arm round Melissa's shoulders; Iris and Jack were hand in hand. The four of them stopped to lean on the gate and gaze along the valley as it lay sleeping in the frosty moonlight.

'Another year almost over,' said Jack, after a long silence.

'Another about to begin,' said Ken.

'Another book to finish,' sighed Melissa.

'Another bout of pneumonia if we hang around,' said Iris

from the depths of her hooded cloak. 'I'm going indoors. Coming, Jack?'

'Sure.'

'How about you two?'

Ken gave Melissa's shoulder a squeeze. 'I think we'd be *de trop*,' he whispered in her ear.

'So would they,' she whispered back. For the time being, they remained where they were and admired the moon.

BETTY ROWLANDS

EXHAUSTIVE ENQUIRIES

'Melissa Craig . . . is an engaging, human heroine'
Financial Times

'The gently old-fashioned style of unravelling the mystery is as riveting as any violent fast-paced novel or film'
Cotswold Life

'Betty Rowlands has that rare skill that grabs the reader's attention at page one and holds it to the end'
Wilts & Gloucestershire Standard

The play was the thing wherein Melissa Craig, mystery writer, would catch . . . exactly what?

A 'Pantocrime', she called it, specially commissioned by the local amateur dramatic society.

Setting: An old country house, now a smart hotel for the Perrier'n'Porsche set.

The plot: Very much thickening. Murder Most Foul, in rhyming couplets.

The cast: A self-made tycoon, his expensively-bred would-be fiancée, a librarian (of the distinctly non-mousey persuasion), a spurned suitor, sundry walks-on and rude mechanicals. The odd something that goes bump in the night.

And a body.

But not on the stage, spattered with stage blood.

In the bar cellar. A real-dead corpse with real blood . . .

HODDER AND STOUGHTON PAPERBACKS